Strings

By Sheryle Criswell Sturdevant

Writers Exchange E-Publishing
http://www.writers-exchange.com/

STRINGS
Copyright 2007 Sheryle Criswell Sturdevant
Writers Exchange E-Publishing
PO Box 372
ATHERTON QLD 4883

Published by Writers Exchange E-Publishing
http://www.writers-exchange.com

Cover by: Laura Shinn

ISBN ebook: 9781921314421
    Print: 978-1-922066-18-3

All characters in this book have no existence outside the imagination of the author and have no relation to anyone bearing the same name or names. Any resemblance to individuals known or unknown to the author are purely coincidental.

For all the children who saw too much

What we call the beginning is often the end,

And to make an end is to make a beginning.

The end is where we start from.

T.S. Elliot

CHAPTER I

Sometimes I think about the mornings, gray and wet, and so cold that my breath looked like steam from a pot of hot tea...except there was no hot tea. The mud then was thick from the pre-dawn rain, and seemed to cover everything. But it didn't matter, because the mud was the earth and the earth was life, and anything that reminded us of the living was good. But I'm getting much too far ahead of myself. It's only fair to tell you the beginning, so that you'll know how I got to the end.

#####

My name is Hanna Berkenski, and the day it actually started was the Sabbath, a lovely sunny Friday in November of 1941. It also happened to be my birthday, my fifteenth birthday. I will try to tell you about my family and my home first, so you will know that in spite of the awful German soldiers who completely took over and ruined our city, we were still a happy home. We were looking forward to the possibility that soon these terrible intruders would go away and let us get back our normal lives.

I was born in a small town in Poland, but to this day, I can't remember the name. When my Papa was able to get his position at the University, we moved to a little house just outside of Warsaw. It was so tiny that my sister

Rachel and I had to share a bed. Sammy, who was the oldest, got to have his own bed, but all of us children slept in the same room.

It wasn't bad to share, except when Sammy ate too much cabbage for dinner...and then he would be very rude...and very smelly. On those particularly bad nights, Rachel and I would take our blankets and pil-

1

lows, and sleep in the parlor, leaving Sammy to deal with his odors all by himself.

The best part about our house was the garden. Mama had a wonderful green thumb, and everything she planted turned into color, which made the house look like something out of a fairy tale. A little cottage surrounded by sparkling multi-colored jewels. In the spring and summer when the breezes blew the lace curtains, and the geraniums and petunias were in bloom, I couldn't imagine anywhere more beautiful.

That all changed soon after my birthday in 1939. My thirteenth birthday was one of the most special days in my life. Mama made dinner for all of my friends, and then we had a magnificent peach cobbler for dessert. Everyone brought me presents, and Papa played the violin and he was quite good. I started my lessons when I was eleven, and while I was making very nice progress, I certainly was no match for my Papa.

I was at the age then where friends become you're whole life. My best friend, Freyda, and I spent practically every spare moment together. We would talk of our special dreams and of the wonderful holidays we would take as soon as we finished school. I would tell her about my plan to become a professor like my father, and while everyone else in my family laughed at the prospect of a woman sitting in a professor's chair, Freyda never laughed. She only said, "We can do anything we want to, Hanna."

Freyda didn't have as lofty ambitions as I did. Her heart's desire was to marry Sig Krazinski and have lots and lots of babies. The only part she left out was that Sig Krazinski had never spoken a single word to her...ever. In fact, he never looked at her, or any other girl for that matter. I always wondered about Sig Krazinski...

Men certainly were not a part of my plan for a long while. I enjoyed the idea of having some handsome young man pay for my dinner, or take me to the theatre. I had no intention of forsaking my dreams for a life of dirty diapers. Not for a long, long time. But, there was this one boy who always smiled at me in class, and I often wondered what it would be like to kiss him. I wondered what it would be like to kiss anyone.

One day, when Freyda and I went down to the lake to sun ourselves, we talked about what it would be like. We decided to try it out on each other...just to see what someone else's lips felt like. We giggled a lot at the thought, but then we tried. It felt soft and warm and nice. But there was something missing. We both felt it. I would never get the answer to the missing part of the puzzle until many years and many sorrows later. When I finally found out that secret, I was no longer the same innocent child who experimented by the lake.

Our life was perfect, from a thirteen-year-old's point of view, until the day the letter came.

It said we were being evicted from our home, because of the War, and all Jews were going to be given housing in Warsaw.

Papa ranted and raved for three days, while Mama went about the unpleasant business of packing up a whole family, a whole life, into cardboard boxes in preparation for our move. We tried to help her with the packing, but she insisted on doing it alone, and every time I looked at her, she had tears running down her cheeks.

I finally managed to talk Mama into allowing me to help. She looked so tired and so sad, I couldn't let her do anymore of it alone.

"Please Mama," I said, "it's too much...please let me help you."

3

She looked into my eyes and enfolded me in her arms, and I could feel her warm tears on my face.

"Why are you crying, Mama?"

"Because we are leaving this house where we have been so happy...where Rachel was born. Because we are leaving my beautiful garden. Because we are being made to live in a ghetto in the middle of our own city, a ghetto surrounded by fences, and walls and locked gates...and soldiers with guns. Why? Because we are Jews? Have we done anything to hurt these people? We have only tried to live by God's laws, to be kind and generous, to love our children, to love our country. That is why I am crying, my Hanna, because I fear this is only the first stop on a much longer and more difficult journey." She said this as she looked deep into my eyes, willing me to understand.

"What journey, Mama? What are you talking about," I asked.

"A journey to the unknown, my darling...a journey that Jews have been taking over and over since Moses led us through the desert. But this time, I fear, there will be no Moses to part the Red Sea."

I remember looking at her, still not knowing the meaning of her words, but the sound of them gave me a chill that went all the way up my spine.

She kissed me then, and said, "Now, get the candlesticks and wrap them carefully in the lace tablecloth."

#####

As soon as I entered the door to our new home, I knew we would all hate that place. The first thing to greet us was the smell. An awful combination of fried fish, boiled cabbage, tobacco smoke, and sewage. What amazed me in the two years that we spent there, was how quickly we got used to those obnoxious odors, until we literally didn't know they existed. Unfortunately,

4

the second thing to greet us was something we never quite got used to...the cockroaches.

We figured out, after not too long, that the only way to survive them was to laugh about them, and eventually, even though they were loathsome, disgusting, sneaky creatures...we began to give them names and track their comings and goings. The only one in our family who enjoyed their presence was Sunshine, our large, mostly orange Tabby cat. Because she was used to being outdoors all the time and was now confined to this tiny torture chamber with five humans, she spent much of her time hunting down the roaches to assuage her boredom.

We tried to think of all the names of people we disliked, like Mr. Schultzkoff, the tailor, or Hirschel Rosenbaum, the bratty boy in Rachel's class at school. And then, when Sunshine reigned victorious in her quest for a particular cockroach, we would laugh and say, "Good! It served him right!"

It took Mama one whole week of scrubbing her fingers raw, to make our new home clean enough to meet her standards. Only when everything finally shined and every corner was scrutinized for dust and crumbs, did she pronounced it our new home. And, announced that we were going to add another member to our family in five months.

There was always a sadness about Mama in those months. I am certain that it was because she heard rumors of what the Germans were doing to the Jews of Europe. And while we all believed, at least in the beginning, that the rumors were silly lies told by half-witted people, and this awful apartment was only temporary, and that we would all be going back to our lovely little house any day. Mama knew in her heart that this was only the beginning of much worse things to come.

The grown-ups in the neighborhood were very careful not to talk in front of the children about the details of these secret and scary things. And so, we were very sheltered from the realities that surrounded us. Of course, we saw the soldiers on the street corners as we made our way to and from school, and as the months went on, there was never enough food. But, because we were young, we took these things in our stride and went about the adventure of living with an indifference that only children can have.

The boundaries of the Warsaw Ghetto, as it was called, were patrolled by German soldiers twenty-four hours a day, seven days a week, so that if anyone was brave enough, or perhaps, stupid enough to try and sneak out...well, it was usually their last stupidly, brave act.

After a while we became used to life as it was, and soon our cramped, little apartment was the only home we thought of.

Five months to the day from Mama's grand announcement, Esther was born. She was named after Papa's father Ezra who died before the War. She was such a beautiful baby that none of us could keep our hands off of her. Rachel, who was eleven at the time, used to carry her around all day long, which was just fine with Mama, who had her hands full enough with taking care of the house, and the cooking, and the laundry.

My job was to help Mama with preparing the meals and with washing the diapers, which as you can imagine, was not my favorite pastime. I particularly hated the winter, when I needed to hang the diapers on a clothesline in the freezing temperatures. When it was time to pull the line in, the diapers would be stiff as boards from the ice, and I nursed hands that were bright red and chapped all winter. I asked Mama what the point was of hanging clothes on the line if they were only going to get frozen. And she said, "The point is, my darling, no one has invented a better way. So unless you are the inventor, we do it this way." How could you argue with that?

And so our lives continued for the next two years. Soon we were not allowed to attend school any longer, and there were endless lines for everything from bread to turnips. We no longer ate eggs, or milk, or meat, or poultry of any kind unless one made a deal with the Devil himself for a tough piece of beef or a scrawny chicken on a special occasion.

And that takes us to the real beginning of my story. We didn't need to deal with the Devil that day...only Mr. Frankel, the butcher. He was the one who provided us with the chicken we had to celebrate my birthday.

CHAPTER II

"Mama, the chicken smells so wonderful," said Rachel, my thirteen year old, whiny sister who was setting the table much too slowly. "I don't think I can wait for dinner. I'm starving to death."

Mama laughed, "To death? You poor deprived child. Well, I guess you will just have to wait another hour until your Papa and Sammy get home."

I loved when Mama laughed in those days, she did it so rarely, and when she did, her whole face lit up, and her eyes sparkled. I continued mashing the potatoes and waited to see what Rachel would do next.

Not to disappoint me, Rachel groaned and began to whine again. "An hour? How can I wait an hour when my stomach is growling like Mrs. Hirschfield's dog?"

"So, if you're so starving, why don't you take a little piece of bread and be glad it is there to be had. A lot of our neighbors don't even have a piece of bread tonight."

"Are you sure, Mama?" asked Rachel. "Usually you're so fussy about..."

Mama put her hands on her hips and scowled at Rachel as I turned away so as not to burst out laughing. "Oh, now I have to listen to a fresh mouth besides? Cut, cut already, things are too difficult around here to worry about a morsel of bread. We'll say the prayer with whatever is left. God will understand."

And then she left the kitchen to check on two-year-old, Esther, who was sleeping in the bedroom and just recovering from a nasty bout with the croup. Esther turned out to be a sickly child, picking up every germ to make its way through the Ghetto. Germs, unlike food, were definitely something that were not in short supply. She slept in an old crib in Mama and Papa's bedroom.

Rachel and Sam and I slept on a high-riser and a cot in what had been a sitting room at one time. The only place we had to sit now as a family, was the kitchen. That was my favorite room anyway. It certainly was the warmest room in the tiny apartment, and it was the only room where the smell from Mama's cooking could drown out the other lingering odors in that old, dilapidated building.

It was also a wonderful place to escape to on the nights when Sammy started passing gas. I once asked Mama if there was something wrong with Sammy that he had to smell up the night all the time. Her answer was, "No, Hanna, he is a perfectly normal man." I guess that explained that.

"RACHEL BERKENSKI..." shouted Mama, as she re-entered the kitchen. "I said a little piece...you don't know from a little? That bread has to last all weekend."

"I'm sorry, Mama," said Rachel as she put part of her bread back on the plate and recovered the plate with the Sabbath cloth. She continued to place the silverware around the table and continued to chatter. "Mama, Sammy is lucky, isn't he?"

"Why lucky?" asked Mama as she filled the water glasses.

"Because he gets to go to Shul with Papa. I wish I could go. I heard Mr. Gutstein say that God is only in the Shul."

I really despised Simon Gutstein. He was a crabby, old man who never had a smile or a nice word for anyone. And he seemed to take great pleasure in teasing children, especially little girls. It always got my blood to boiling when I saw him making snide remarks and ridiculous faces at the girls on the street.

"What," I said, "it's such a blessing to sit in a room with a bunch of smelly, old men who don't know from soap and tooth powder? You want to pray? You can pray right here in your own house. God is everywhere, Rachel. He is in this kitchen, and he is in the closet, and he is even down the hall in the washroom. Anywhere you want him to be, he is there. Don't you believe that Simon Gutstein when he tells you God is only in the room with men. God made us too, you know, he isn't so stupid that he only talks to the ones with whiskers."

"Your sister is right, Rachel," Mama added. "Simon Gutstein should keep his mouth shut more often. Now, will you please speed yourself up a bit so we can finish before Papa gets home. This is a special night, a special Shabbat for our Hanna."

"I know, I just wish we could have a cake for her birthday like we used to," said Rachel.

"If _ifs_ were horses, my darling Rachel, then beggars would be riding and poor Jewish families would have chickens every night," replied Mama.

Mama had lots of tidbits of wisdom, one or more for every occasion.

"Mama," I asked, as I put the candlesticks on the table and readied them for Mama's blessing, "how did you get the chicken for our dinner tonight? It's been such a long time since we had a roasted chicken. I can hardly remember what it tastes like, and nobody gets chickens anymore unless they..."

"SHHH..." Mama said putting her finger to her lips. "I went to Mr. Frankel. He owed me a big favor from when his wife had the baby. I went every day to help her, remember? And no small job either, I can tell you, that boy of hers, Henrik, what a handful, two handfuls

10

maybe. With a new baby and that child, poor Bella must be nipping at the schnapps during nap times."

Mama had a very funny sense of humor too, and we loved to listen and laugh when she told a story. "So," she continued. "Mr. Frankel says, 'if I you need something, you should come to me. I have connections'."

"Connections?" Rachel and I asked at the same time, which made us laugh again.

"Do I know?" said Mama. "I don't ask. I need a chicken for Hanna's birthday, I go to Frankel...I say 'chicken'. He says, 'Good as done'...and POOF! like magic."

"A chicken..." we all said in unison and then laughed loudly yet again.

"Yes, a plump, beautiful, fresh chicken and with the giblets even," said Mama.

"Do you know where he got it?" I asked.

"I don't know, I don't ask, I don't care," said Mama as she put up her hands in a gesture of surrender.

Of course, Rachel couldn't let it go at that and she insisted, "I'll bet you know, you just don't want to tell us because we're children. Why are you grown-ups always so secretive? I'm not a baby anymore, you know. For heaven's sake, I'm almost old enough to get married."

At that, Mama and I completely dissolved into fits of laughter, which only made Rachel angrier.

"Old enough to get married?" laughed Mama. "And who do you think will marry you when they find out your Mama still cooks all your food and washes all your clothes. And if that isn't enough, it takes you all afternoon to set a Shabbat table?"

Being somewhat humbled by Mama's kidding, Rachel quickly finished setting the table as she spoke to herself out loud thinking we didn't hear, but of course we did. "Well, you could still tell me some things, sometime. I'm not exactly an infant, you know..."

"Very well," said Mama, "I will tell you something right now." Both Rachel and I stopped doing our chores and turned to Mama expecting some grand and important pronouncement.

"Really?" said Rachel, as she looked at Mama with great anticipation. "What are you going to tell me?"

"Now that you are done setting a lovely Shabbat table for Hanna's fifteenth birthday, now, you can go wash the radishes. How is that?"

Rachel stomped her foot and ran to the sink, mumbling and grumbling the entire time. In order to diffuse a situation, which could only get worse, I said, "Mama, unless you need me for something else right now, would you mind if I practiced a bit before Papa and Sammy get home?"

"Absolutely, Hanna, go practice. I love to hear you play. You know, Hanna, how sorry we are that you cannot take lessons any longer."

"I know, Mama, I'll take lessons after the War. And for now, Papa is teaching me and he's very good, even if he does get a little crabby sometimes."

"Well, you know what a perfectionist he is, if you make a mistake, it drives him crazy. Just listen, do what you can, and try to ignore his nit-picking."

I just smiled, dried my hands, and went into the used-to-be sitting room, which was now my shared bedroom. I retrieved my violin case from the shelf above my bed and took out my lovely violin. I was so proud to now own this beautiful, old instrument, which had belonged to my grandfather. I wasn't quite sure how old it was, but it was very used. I kept it polished to a high shine, and I was very diligent about replacing the strings when they became the slightest bit worn.

Of all the things I enjoyed in my life at fifteen, playing the violin was perhaps my favorite. Sometimes when I was able to get into the moment especially well, I'd play a whole piece without a single mistake. And when I'd finished, I would sit back and think: *Was that really me playing so beautifully?*

I took out my violin, dusted it carefully with the skirt of my apron, and began to play the opening bars of the Merry Widow Waltz, one of my favorites.

CHAPTER III

The banging on the door shocked us all into silence. I put down my violin and walked to Mama, who was standing dead still in front of the door. Rachel dropped the radishes and the knife into the sink and slowly walked to Mama too. The knocking came again, only louder this time, and with it came a strange and angry voice, one that spoke Polish with a very bad accent.

"OPEN THIS DOOR!" shouted the voice.

Mama looked from me to Rachel and then answered quietly, "Who is there?"

"Open this door by order of the Fuehrer and the Third Reich, or we will force it open!" shouted the voice again.

"It will be all right, girls, it will be fine," whispered Mama as she went to open the door a crack.

As if the crack in the door were an invitation, the door was pushed open with such force that Mama was thrown back and would have fallen if I hadn't grabbed her. I looked up and saw every European Jew's worst nightmare during World War II...Nazi SS soldiers, two of them. One was holding a rifle, which was pointed directly at us. The taller of the two looked to be in his thirties perhaps, and was rather nice looking in a stern and stiff sort of way. The shorter one holding the rifle, could not have been much older than I, and appeared to be very angry and very nervous.

"Put down the gun, Klaus, they will give us no trouble," said the older of the two as he turned to Mama. "Woman, where is your husband?"

"He went to pray," said Mama, "I expect him home any minute for the Sabbath meal."

The young one named Klaus, began walking around the dining table, still holding the rifle, and he started to laugh. "These crazy Jews and their barbaric rituals," he said, as he threw the bread cover aside and tore off a large hunk of our Challah bread. He then went to the other end of the table, lifted the carafe of sweet wine, drank deeply, and then wiped his mouth with the end of Mama's beautiful antique laced tablecloth that had belonged to her grandmother.

Growing impatient with the younger man's folly, the taller soldier finally ordered, "Leave that, will you! We have more important things to do. Go check the rest of this place to see if there is anyone else."

Klaus laughed again and went out toward the bedroom, as the other took out a folded paper from his pocket that contain a long list of names.

"What is your name, woman?" he asked.

"It is Berkenski, Miriam Berkenski," said Mama.

"Berkenski...Berkenski...I know that name from a long time ago, I think..." he said as he went down the list of B names. "And your husband's name?"

"Meyer, Meyer Berkenski," said Mama. "And how could you know us? I don't remember you. What is your name? And what is it that you want from us?"

"It is of no importance now what my name is or how I know you. And furthermore, Miriam Berkenski, it is none of your damn business what we want with you. Do you understand that?" he replied with such venom that Mama backed away.

"And who are these?" he asked as he pointed to Rachel and me.

"They are my daughters, Rachel, who is thirteen and Hanna, who is fifteen today," Mama answered.

15

"So, Berkenskis, we have come to collect you and the rest of your neighbors, and see that you are transported to a relocation center here in Poland and..."

"What is a relocation center? What does that mean?" Mama interrupted, not even realizing that she was being a little too brave.

"It means, that you and your daughters and your neighbors are Jews. And who else lives here with you?"

"My son, Samuel, he lives here also," said Mama.

"Uh huh, you did not mention this son before. Why is that, Miriam?" he asked, not really expecting an answer.

Rachel, of course, could not keep still any longer and asked, "But where is this place we're going?"

"It is a work camp, and then we will decide what to do with you," he answered.

"But, why can't we stay here?" she persisted.

"My, my, you are a nosey little bitch, huh?" he laughed. "And your answer is, because you are not welcome in this city anymore. Do you understand that? Jews are not welcome anywhere anymore. That is what our Fuehrer has said. Now, you have your answer, little girl, are you satisfied?"

"Work camp?" said Mama. "There are rumors of such places, that they are dirty, and that Jews are not treated well, that some are even killed... What is this place?"

And then I knew, in that second, I knew what Mama had been brooding about for the past two years. She heard stories that had not gotten to our ears, tales of terrible places where Jews were treated more like animals than humans. She worried about our fate for two years in silence, and now her worst fears were being realized. I put my arms around her and held her close

16

and felt the warm tears again on my face, as I had when we first came to this awful place to live. The only difference, this time they were Mama's tears mixed with my own.

"Now, get your things together quickly. Do you think we have all day to stand and chat with the likes of you?" said the soldier with a sneer. It was hard to know just why he was so angry with us. We hadn't done anything to arouse his anger and yet he continued to shout at us and call us vulgar names.

Rachel and Mama started to cry again just as the younger soldier re-entered the kitchen. He walked to the other and whispered in his ear, "There is a child in there, Lieutenant Rovling," and he pointed to the bedroom.

The Lieutenant turned to him abruptly and said so quietly that only I could hear, "Don't say my name again in front of this woman. Do you understand?" Then he turned back to Mama.

"A child," he said, with a nasty, gleeful lift to his voice, "my, my, my, Miriam Berkenski, shame on you. Did you think you could fool us?"

"No, I wasn't trying..."

"Then why didn't you tell me about the child?"

"She was asleep," pleaded Mama. "She is sick with the croup, and so little. I simply did not think to..."

"You simply did not think, period," growled the soldier, who I knew, at this point, was an officer, and who somehow knew my family. "NOW GO, get your things together and hurry! We must leave here!"

I am sure that Rachel was even more scared than Mama and I, maybe because she was younger, and maybe because her personality never allowed her to see any evil in the world. She turned to Mama and said, "Mama, what about Papa and Sammy?"

17

"Yes, yes, my husband, he will be home any moment, and my son. Can't we wait just until they arrive?"

The more Mama spoke, the angrier he became, and the more hysterical she became, until she was actually pleading with this inhuman monster in polished boots. "Please, please, sir, I can't leave without them, can't you understand? Surely, you must have a family...children. Could you leave without them? I can't, it's not possible for that to happen. I must wait..."

"YOU MUST SHUT YOUR MOUTH!" he shouted at the top of his lungs as he grabbed her by the arms and shouted into her face once again. "YOU HAVE NO CHOICE, STUPID WOMAN. NOW GO AND GET YOUR THINGS!" He then flung her aside as if she were a rag doll.

In what was to become a journey of courage, Mama stood up and faced the demon again. "But my baby, my Esther, she is so sick. You must see that I can not take her out in the night air."

He grabbed her by the neck this time and spit the words in her face. "Then you will leave her!"

"NO!!!" roared Mama as she backed away from him. "I can't leave my child. Is your heart made of stone?"

This time when he spoke, it was scarier than all the times before, because this time, as he grabbed her arms again, he whispered in her ear, "I told you to shut your mouth, bitch. I will tell you one more time, get your things now or I will shut your mouth for you. The child will be sent to you later with your husband and son."

Mama pulled away again and as she rubbed her bruised arms she muttered under her breath, "Liar!"

With that one word, the one named Klaus ran forward and seized Mama by the hair. Rachel let out a scream and I held her, because I didn't know what else to do.

"I heard that, Jew," he hissed in his snake-like way. "You heard the Lieutenant. Get your things or I will drag you from this disgusting hovel with nothing but the clothes on your back. Maybe you will freeze to death, and then we won't have to waste any more time on you."

By this time, Rachel was sobbing loudly. The soldier let go of Mama and turned his attention to Rachel. I tried to protect her, but he shoved me out of the way as he pulled her to him.

"Stop your hysterics, you filthy little Kike, or I will personally take great pleasure in wringing your skinny neck while your mother watches your last breath. Or, maybe I will even do worse to this beautiful, little body. Huh, Mama?" And then he laughed and laughed...and laughed.

"ENOUGH!" shouted the other, the one called Lieutenant.

Wiping her eyes and trying to regain some semblance of dignity, Mama asked, "What can we bring with us?"

"Take anything of value...coins, silver, jewelry," he said.

"May we take clothing, and my bible, my photographs?"

"Yes, yes, just hurry!" he snapped.

For the next ten minutes, Mama and Rachel and I gathered our possessions in what looked like a ballet of horror. We moved in silence and willed our legs to keep us going out of sheer terror. Rachel and I went about the job of filling our small suitcases with clothes. Mama gathered her precious bible, her family photographs, and her beautiful brass candlesticks, which she rolled in the lace tablecloth, just as we had done when we left our little house in the country, and moved to this Hell.

When we came out of the bedroom areas with our suitcases and coats, I saw Mama do one last thing. She took the small wooden box from on top of the sideboard and lifted the lid. From inside, she took out the string of perfectly matched pearls Papa had given her on her wedding day, and a lovely old cameo brooch, which was the only thing left of her mother. She held them to her breast for a moment and closed her eyes, and then she replaced the brooch in the box, fastened the pearls around her neck, and carefully put the box inside the carpetbag with the rest of her treasures.

All the while the two SS soldiers walked around the apartment impatiently. The one called Klaus stopped by my bed and lifted the violin I had left there.

"What is this?" he asked.

"It is a violin," I said. "What does it look like?"

"Oh, such a smart-mouth Jew, huh? Do you play this?"

"I do."

He looked at the other, and the two men silently seemed to be exchanging information, then the Lieutenant said, "Take this with you, girl." He picked up the case, took the violin from Klaus, and thrust them both at me.

As I put my beloved violin away in its case, Mama and Rachel went in to see Esther before we had to leave.

I said my good-byes to my sleeping little sister when I had gone to get Mama's few clothes and her coat. I remember standing over her crib and thinking I would probably never see her again. Surprisingly, I couldn't cry over that. Perhaps it was because I was so numbed

20

by what was happening or maybe it was because I really believed that when we left, Papa and Sammy would come home and take her to safety.

I leaned over the crib rails and kissed her gently on the cheek, being very careful not to wake her, and for just a moment, I felt more love for this tiny child than I had ever felt for anyone or anything in all my life.

As I gathered up our bags and put on my coat with the yellow Star of David on the front, I was sure I could overhear a conversation between the two men. Of course, I pretended not to hear, but I could make out enough of what they said to know.

"Why are you being so delicate with this woman?" asked Klaus. "You could shoot them all right here and be done with it."

"Her husband, Meyer Berkenski, was my professor at the University. I had come here on an exchange program for one year. She gave me dinner once when I was a poor student. She doesn't recognize my face," the Lieutenant replied. "I need to give them, at least, a chance." And I could see by the look on his face that he was, indeed, in conflict as to how to handle Miriam Berkenski and her daughters.

Then, something happened that chilled me to the bone, words I have not forgotten in all these sixty years. The Lieutenant leaned in close to Klaus and said, "See to the child."

"With pleasure, Lieutenant."

And then the Lieutenant whispered, still loud enough for me to understand, "And remember, Klaus, they are all vermin, the small as well as the big. If you let one live, then the disease continues to spread. Remember why we are here. Neither of us must allow sentimentality to cloud our reason. Now, let's get them out of here."

21

Apparently, in just those few seconds, the Lieutenant had decided that a meal from a Jew was not worth saving her life.

With that, Klaus began to shout, "IT IS TIME...LET'S GO..."

Mama and Rachel came running from the bedroom and Mama said, "Please don't shout, let her sleep at least." And of course, this simple request brought more abuse, as Klaus shoved her toward the door.

"Will we be back after the War, Mama?" asked Rachel as she struggled to get her heavy suitcase out of the door, "because I didn't get a chance to say good-bye to Jiri, and my other friends at school. And my cat, Mama, who will feed her when she comes home?"

"MOVE!" shouted Klaus again.

"Please, please tell my husband that we will see him later and please take care not to wake Esther and if the cat comes home..." Mama begged as she headed out of the door for the last time. We then noticed that only the Lieutenant was coming with us, Klaus was staying behind. And again I knew.

"Get going, damn you and your demands," the Lieutenant shouted as he shoved us toward the stairs. He stopped, turned back to Klaus, and whispered again, this time in a voice just barely loud enough for all of us to hear, "And if their stinking feline returns..."

"Don't worry, Sir," said Klaus, "I will see to both the child and the animal." Then he laughed and laughed and laughed. That is what we heard going down the stairs and out into the street of the Warsaw Ghetto on that night in November of 1941. That, and the sound of Esther screaming...

CHAPTER IV

I don't remember much about the walk to the large truck that night, except for the number of people in the street, and the screaming that followed me as we left the building. It seemed as though the whole neighborhood was being emptied, all at the same time. The street swarmed with Jews, as old and young alike were herded like cattle, by the Nazi soldiers at gun point, into the big caravan of trucks that would take us all to the train. Of course, at the time, we knew nothing of the trains, we only saw the putrid green transports, and that was enough to cause whimpers of fear from the people whose fates had yet to be determined.

Mama, Rachel, and I were shoved into one of the trucks, and as I looked around, I saw Mrs. Steiner, looking very old and sickly, and Mrs. Frankel with all of her six children, and Mrs. Gutstein who was all crippled with arthritis. Except for the very old and the very young, there were hardly any men, because they were all in Shul on this Friday, the day of my birthday. A day I would never, never forget.

The truck started to move and within half an hour, it stopped at the Central Railroad Station in the middle of downtown Warsaw. I knew the station well because we had taken the train from there many times to visit Mama's sister in the village of Lowicz.

How I loved the trips to Auntie Ada's, and her sparkling white house set in the middle of jewel-colored gardens. Just past the stand of trees at the rear of her house, was Lake Lazenki, which had the same name as the famous park in Warsaw. When I was very small, Papa and I would walk down to the crystal clear lake and wade to our ankles in the frosty water, and then we would hunt for beautiful stones along the banks. Papa would always try to fish, telling me how wonderful our dinner would be with fresh bass from the lake, sauteed in butter until the skins were crispy and the meat as white as snow. I would sit and watch him, every single time, and listen to his menus and my mouth would water with anticipation. And all he ever caught were tiny minnows that wouldn't even make a mouthful. I loved our time by the lake anyway.

As I jumped from the truck carrying my heavy valise and my violin case, I couldn't help wondering if I would ever see Lowicz and Lake Lazenki again.

Then the shouting and the insults began again:

"HURRY UP, HURRY! YOU PEOPLE ARE TOO SLOW."

"SWINE! THAT'S WHAT YOU ARE, NO BETTER THAN SWINE."

"FILTHY JEWS! LOOK AT YOU IN YOUR FILTHY RAGS."

"HOW COULD GOD HAVE MADE SUCH A MISTAKE AS YOU?"

And on and on it went as they shoved us, en mass, along the tracks to the train. In my innocence, I had imagined we would all be on passenger cars, perhaps three to a seat since there were so many of us, but at least we would be allowed to sit in a car with windows and fresh air. How wrong I was again!

As the Nazi soldiers stopped the crowd, they began pushing people up into cars with huge sliding doors. These were the same cars used to carry cattle before the War, and now, they were carrying Jews to mysterious places, where unknown things would happen to us.

As we stood waiting our turn to be sent into the cars, Rachel turned to me and said, "Hanna, look, that little girl over there. She looks just like Leah Gorski."

24

And then she turned to Mama and said again, "Mama, look that must be Leah Gorski over there, see? I think she's lost, I have to go help her." With that she broke away from us and started to push her way through the crowd. Without thinking there were guns pointed directly at us, Mama went after her and caught her by the arm before any of the soldiers noticed what was happening.

"NO, Rachel, no, it is not Leah. Can't you see?" said Mama, with panic in her voice. "She is much too small, that girl, and she doesn't look at all like Leah. Please, Rachel, please behave. She will be taken care of. We must think of ourselves now, we can not give them any reason to notice us."

Rachel was beyond reason that day, whether from fear or from an overwhelming need to do something to stop what was happening. "But, Mama, she is lost and scared, we have to help."

"We are all lost and scared, my Rachel."

"But, Mama, who are all these people, there are so many?"

"They are our neighbors, they are Jews like us, there are others too. They are all being relocated, their names are on the list."

"There is a list?" asked Rachel.

"From the looks of this rail station, I would say a very long one," answered Mama, and then she gently led Rachel back to our place in line just as one of the soldiers told us to throw our bags up into the train car.

"I want to hold my bag, Mama. Don't let them take it, I need to hold my bag," Rachel cried as she hugged her suitcase tight to her body. Her pleading cries, unfortunately, attracted exactly the attention Mama was trying to avoid, and one of the Nazi soldiers rushed over and grabbed Mama by the arm.

"OW! You're hurting me," cried Mama as she tried to pull away from his grasp.

The soldier, who looked to me like a twin of that other awful man, Klaus, started to yell at Mama. "Shut up and get in that car!" And then he shoved her hard and made her climb up into the boxcar.

"Now you!" he shouted at Rachel, "Drop that bag on the ground!"

When she wouldn't let go, he grabbed the suitcase away from her with such force that I had to keep her from falling over in the swarm of people. He threw her case to the ground and stomped on it and shouted again, "GET UP THERE, GIRL!"

"I can't, I can't reach it," whined Rachel, and to tell you the truth, at that moment, I could have strangled her for being such a baby. All she managed to accomplish was to bring two other soldiers running. All three of them shouted in German for a second and then two of the soldiers grabbed her arms and literally, threw her up into the rail car and into my Mama's arms. The third soldier picked up her suitcase and threw it into the car after her.

As I was being shoved into the car after Rachel, I saw two of the young soldiers walk away laughing. One of them said to the other, "Disgusting! Jew stink all over my hands!" And then, they laughed again, as they wiped their hands on each other like silly schoolboys.

As I stood in the doorway of the train car looking out over the sea of faces, I couldn't help wondering what this was all for. Why would they put themselves to so much trouble to round up all of us Jews, and the Catholics priests, and the blind old men, and babies too young to even see? What harm did these people cause that would make them enemies of Germany? And now, where are they taking us all?

26

CHAPTER V

The darkness rolled in that night like a blanket thrown over the world. As the train readied to pull out of the Central Railroad Station, the great wooden doors were slammed shut, blocking out all but slivers of light from the lampposts. Little specks of light that found their way through the slats in the boxcar siding cast an eerie glow on the already distorted faces of my traveling companions. When the train engine began to roar and the whistle blew, denoting our departure, all of the light disappeared in a few seconds throwing my world into total blackness. It was as if the earth had dropped out from under us and we were being hurled through space...totally out of control.

In the background, there were murmurs of grief, and cries from hungry babies, and prayers. On this trip, there would be endless, unceasing prayers.

Except for my mother and Rachel, I cannot tell you who stood near me that night, it was too dark to see faces. The body heat became unbearable after a few hours, in spite of the cold temperatures, and it didn't take long before the car reeked with the stench of urine, and faeces, and vomit.

Mama suggested we drop our cases to the floor and sit on them, and we were only too happy to oblige.

Rachel, overcome with the shock of this terrible ordeal, was still able to find a bit of energy with which to complain.

"Mama, it's so crowded in here," she whimpered. "I can't move, there are people pressing against me on every side, and it smells disgusting."

Mama, at the end of her patience, snapped back, "Rachel, enough! Stop your complaining! We are all in the same uncomfortable condition. Can't you see that? You are no worse off than any others here. Look around you."

"But, Mama," Rachel persisted, "I can't breathe. Do these people ever bathe?"

"Rachel, do you suppose that the Nazis are in the habit of allowing the Jews to bathe and perfume themselves before dragging them off to the trains?"

"Well, I don't like it! And I'm scared."

"I know you don't," said Mama, more gently now, as she touched Rachel's cheek. "We are all frightened, but we have to be brave. We can all do that for a while, can't we? We must be brave and strong so Papa will be proud of us."

"Mama," I said, "the soldier told us we are going to a work camp. What will we do there?"

Mama chuckled a little. "Well, we will work, I presume. Maybe they will have us cooking in the kitchen or caring for the children. Cooking wouldn't be so bad, huh? Plenty of food and cooking is something we all know how to do. Papa, maybe they will have Papa teach the children to read and write. The children still must learn while we are being relocated, right? And Sammy, Sammy is strong. Maybe they will have him building things."

"And where will we live?" I asked.

"I haven't the slightest idea, Hanna, but I am sure we will be able to survive it. Of course, it will not be comfortable like our little house, but it can't be much worse than that horrid apartment in Warsaw, huh? I mean, after all, these Nazis are still human, aren't they, even if they are a little crazy?" And then she laughed. It was good to hear her laugh. But, it sounded dreadfully out of place.

"And what if we can never go home?" asked Rachel.

28

"NO! That will not happen," scolded Mama. "We will go home! All of us, Papa, Sammy, Esther, and us, we will go home and be a family again. Then life will be good like it always was in our little house, with my beautiful garden. And, after the War, things will be better, better than even before. There will be chickens for dinner, and shoes, and cough medicine for Esther. We will have these things, all of them, after the War, because Mr. Roosevelt has said everything will be fine. I heard this from Mrs. Nussberg, when her son wrote to her from America and said it was so."

We were silent then and sat crushed to near immobility for a long time. We listened to the sounds around us, an old man's breathing, a mother singing a lullaby to a terrified child, a father praying on this Sabbath for the safety of his children.

Then quite unexpectedly, we heard another sound mixed with the sobbing and sadness. It was the absurd sound of laughter, not laughter like Mama's before, but the cackling laughter of a twisted mind. It was the sound of a single voice laughing at some private joke, and it sounded as if it were right behind us.

I looked around, trying to see where the voice was coming from, but in the blackness of the boxcar I could not pick out a solitary face. Soon the laughing voice began to fade and was replaced by a speaking voice that was far more frightening than the absurd laughing.

"False hopes from America. Denial! It is denial, you fools. Mr. Roosevelt, the great American, he sits in his fancy office, wearing his fine woolen suit, and eating beef, and he tells us how things will be better. And you believe this nonsense. You are not only fools but you are stupid besides, because Mr. Roosevelt closes his eyes to what is happening to the Jews. All of them, all of those rich American men in their gray flannel suits -

29

they sit in their lavish offices sipping Sherry, and smoking cigars, and they do not lift a finger to end this outrage. They do not even attempt to squash the madmen, to save the Jews. They are no better than these Nazis, their hands also have blood on them, only that blood cannot be seen. They fill their fat bellies with meat, and potatoes, and chocolates. Isn't that funny? Why do you not laugh? Chocolates, made by the hands of the very villains here in Europe who are becoming rich on the bodies and souls of your mothers, and your children, and these strangers here around you who reek of pain, and fear, and death."

"STOP!" shouted Mama, who couldn't take another second of this verbal torture.

"What does he mean, Mama?" asked a badly frightened Rachel.

"He means nothing, Rachel," and then she turned in the direction of the voice and spoke in a tone that could only be described as furious. "Some people should mind their own business when there are frightened children around. Some people should keep their opinions to themselves when their words can only cause more suffering."

The laughing came again and the voice continued. "Have it your way. But closing your eyes will not make this horror go away any more than it has done for your precious Americans. The children that you try to protect from my words, may be the only hope that this will never happen again. Let them hear, let them hear what evil there is in the world. Then if they are lucky enough to survive, they will know it, if they ever meet it again, face to face."

I have never forgotten those chilling words, but at the time, Mama wasn't the slightest bit interested in what she called, "the ravings of a lunatic".

"Will you be still," she hissed at him. "Why do you need to make this worse?"

Then Mama turned to us and said, "It will be alright, my daughters. Do you believe me when I tell you something or do you believe a crazy stranger who makes no sense?"

"Yes, Mama, you know we believe you," I said, "but what he says does make some sense to me, and it's very frightening."

"Then don't listen and you will not be frightened," Mama said. "And don't tell me that his babble makes sense to anyone. Not when we sit here like fish to be canned, or like the cattle who rode in this car last week. Even the cows are given food and water. Now, enough of this! Let us talk of only pleasant things that will help us to pass the time and to ease our fears."

"Mama, can you tell me a story, like when I was little?" asked Rachel.

"Would you like hear one of the fairy stories that I tell to Esther?"

"No, tell us about Papa."

Mama chuckled, "Papa...what would you like to know?"

"How old were you when you met him?" I asked.

"I was practically a child, Hanna...only one year older than you are now."

"Mama, I am hardly a child. I can take care of a house all by myself and I even have a boy who is interested in me," I replied in my own defense.

"Well then, my grown-up lady, you will understand that while I was too young to marry, I wasn't too young to be in love."

I couldn't believe that Mama was going to tell us such a private part of her life, but then again, strange situations make for strange conversations. And then she continued...

"In my time, the grown-ups in the Jewish community still believed in arranged marriages. I wasn't too happy about that idea, as you can imagine. But still, they had the old ways and they had no intention of listening to my objections. Things were very different when I was young. Children minded their parents, or they didn't sit too well for many days. Not like you sassy girls," she added with a smile that we couldn't see, but we knew was there, because of the way she squeezed our hands.

"Mama," whined Rachel, "this is 1941, things are different now than in the olden days when you were young."

"Stop being stupid, Rachel," I said, "and let Mama tell her story."

"So anyway," Mama continued again, "they introduced me to your Papa when I was just sixteen, but we didn't marry until I was eighteen. It was a very long courtship."

And then Rachel interrupted again. "Did you love Papa instantly the first time you saw him?"

"My goodness, no...not one bit," said Mama, "I was in love with someone else."

Rachel giggled at the thought of Mama being in love with anyone except Papa...but it made me think about Josef, and how I probably would never see him again. I concentrated on Mama's words so that my thoughts would stay in the present. I knew that if I started to think about my feelings for Josef Weidman, I would never be able to stop the tears.

Mama continued her story. "Oh, don't get me wrong, your Papa was a wonderful looking man, just like today. He was tall and slender with a head full of thick, wavy hair and gentle sad eyes. I liked him very much, but my heart belonged to Franz Hermann and no one else. And, because I was young and with my head full of dreams and my eyes full of stars, I was certain that if I could not marry Franz, then my heart would break right in two."

Yes, Mama, I thought, *I know that exact feeling.* But, what I actually <u>said</u> was, "Is Franz Hermann the same Mr. Hermann from the bookstore?"

"Yes, Hanna, the very same."

"But, Mama, Mr. Hermann isn't Jewish. How could you marry him?"

Mama laughed, but covered her mouth so that none of our fellow travelers would hear. "Hanna, my child, love does not stop to ask first how you worship God. Usually that comes second and then, you have to figure out what to do next."

"So, I guess you never sneaked out to meet him or anything, huh?" asked Rachel, whose mind always seemed to come up with immature questions for everything.

"I should say not, Rachel, your grandfather would not have been amused if I'd been caught in a trick like that. And, my dear, I'm surprised to know you even think of such things."

"Don't be surprised, Mama," I joked. "Rachel has a very sneaky mind."

I think Rachel tried to punch me then, but Mama was sitting close enough to see her swing and grabbed her arm before it landed.

"Let's not have any of that now. It's so crowded in here, Rachel, that you might miss your sister and hit some innocent person by mistake."

"Don't worry, Mama, I have very good aim."

"Do you want to hear the end of my story, or do you want to act like a big baby?"

With that, Rachel settled down and Mama went on with her story. I felt a little better, teasing Rachel had always been one of my favorite and most rewarding pastimes.

"So, to answer your question. Your grandfather was a very strict man. If I had left the house to see a non-Jewish boy...oy...he would have cut off my braids, dressed me in overalls. Then he would have sent me out to work in Mr. Kauffmann's stables so I would smell too bad for any man to be interested in me."

"But that's so mean and old-fashioned, Mama," Rachel remarked, as if she were all that well versed in the new morality of the day.

"Well, maybe so, Miss Modern Woman. I will love to see how you behave when you have children of your own who disobey. Be that as it may...all I could do was to sit in the window seat every afternoon and wait for him to pass by on his way home."

"Home...home from where?" I asked.

Mama chuckled again. "I don't know. Sometimes, I think he passed by every day just to see me. When he walked by he always looked up and smiled and I would wave. Afterward, I would sit there by the window and dream about how we would love each other, and what our children would look like. All this, without ever a thought that it could never happen."

"And when did you stop being in love with Mr. Hermann?" asked Rachel.

Mama hugged us to her and whispered, "When I started being in love with your Papa."

"Well, well, well...isn't that a lovely sentiment." It was the man's voice again, as before. "Yes, a lovely sentimental tale for your children. And where is their Papa

34

now? Woe unto him and all of the husbands who simply went to pray on this historic Shabbat. They all will perish together, while the wives, and the children, and the old people take this train ride. Woe to them, woe to me, woe to all of us."

"Have you nothing better to do than to eavesdrop on other people's private conversations?" Mama snapped back at this voice in the dark.

"You think you can have privacy in here, woman? What a fantasy that is, huh?" continued the voice, completely ignoring Mama's objections. "Privacy is not an abundant commodity at the moment, dear lady, in case you hadn't noticed. Can you not smell the lack of privacy?" And then he laughed his dark laugh that was drowned out by the combined pain of a hundred other voices.

"You are a fool with an empty head if you must intrude into the affairs of others," said Mama in a most unfriendly way.

"Perhaps...perhaps," laughed the voice.

We all sat in silence for a long time then. I could hear the train as it rumbled along the tracks, I could hear the babies whimpering from hunger, and I could hear the old men snoring. I could just make out a few stars through the spaces between the boxcar siding. And, even though I held my handkerchief over my nose, I could still smell the foul air.

My mind began to drift back to Josef. I tried not to let myself think, but it was no use, the ache in my heart for my father, and my brother, and my little sister, was magnified when it was combined with the pain of knowing I would never again see my friends...and my Josef.

I wished I could have told Mama what was in my heart, because I knew she'd understand how leaving

35

Josef made me feel as though I had a huge hole in my heart. I had never felt that pain before; it was so bottomless, so hopeless...so empty. It was the kind of pain one feels only when a loved one dies. And wasn't that, after all, what happened today? We all died, even though we were still breathing. I put my head down to my knees and cried...and cried...and cried.

"Are you all right, Hanna?" whispered Mama as she touched my head with her warm hand.

"No, Mama, I'm not."

She lifted my face and kissed my tear-covered cheeks and whispered again, "I know."

#####

After what seemed like days, but what in truth, was only a few minutes, Mama said, "Tell me, Hanna, what are you thinking?"

I wondered where I should begin. And then, I just began.

"I was thinking of how much I miss Papa, and Sammy, and Esther, and hope they are all safe. I was thinking about how much I will miss my friends; my special, special friends." I had decided to keep Josef to myself for a little while longer. "And I was thinking about what I will do when I get to be an adult."

"Were you? And what have you decided?"

"I have decided that I will go to the University. Of course, all of this awfulness will be over, and Papa will be back to teaching. He and I will meet under the huge Elms in the Commons everyday for lunch. And I will become a great scholar, just like him. I will read the words of Charles Dickens, and O. Henry, and Emily Dickinson, and of course, William Shakespeare."

Mama chuckled a bit at that. "I see, and that is all you will do all day, is read?"

"Oh, no, I will travel. I will travel the whole world, to exotic and far off countries, like China and Africa, and America, the most beautiful country of all."

"And how do you know that America is so beautiful?" asked Mama.

"Because in school we read about New York City. So I know it is an excellent place. I have seen pictures of the Statue of Liberty, and the tallest building in the world called the Empire State Building. And I have also seen pictures of the mountains, and the oceans, and the place called California that is all covered with flowers."

"All covered with flowers? Tell me more about America," urged Mama who seemed genuinely interested in what I had to say, unlike Rachel who kept yawning loudly.

"Well, I have seen other pictures in my geography book, where the streets are sparkling clean and the sun shines every day. And what is best of all, and this is the reason that I will live in America one day, all of the children, Mama, all of the children, run and play in the streets the whole day long. I suppose they have to go to school sometimes, but they all seem so happy. And do you know why they are happy, Mama?" Mama shook her head and I told her. "It is because they are never hungry or afraid. Can you imagine such a place, where no one is ever hungry or afraid?"

"They smile all the time?" asked Rachel after a particularly noisy yawn.

"Yes! And I know this most definitely because I have seen pictures of American people and they are smiling in every one."

"And these pictures of such a perfect world, they are all in your geography book?" Mama asked.

37

"Yes, they are!" I replied. But before I could go on, I was interrupted again by the voice of the crazy man.

"PROPAGANDA!" he bellowed.

Mama was livid that this man would dare to interfere again. "Ignore that ignorant man who would spoil a young girl's dreams."

And then he laughed.

"I'm not listening to him, Mama, because I am very sure of these things. And I have decided, too, what I will do when I go to live in America."

Mama said, "Go on, Hanna, tell me your dream."

"Well, first of all, I will live in a big house with oriental rugs on the floors, and satin draperies on the huge French doors, that look out on green lawns like emeralds and ancient Oak trees. There will be beautiful gardens filled with marigolds, and peonies, and rose bushes in every color imaginable. I will have my breakfast in the gardens in the Summer, and feed the Cardinals with my scraps of toast. There will, of course, be lots of bedrooms so that you and Papa, and Rachel, and Sammy and Esther too, can come and visit any time you like. Maybe, you'll love it so much, that you'll want to move to America. Then you can come and share my house."

I loved this place I had gone to in my mind and I continued to tell Mama and Rachel about my new life in America.

"When I am not going to the museums in New York or shopping on the fine Fifth Avenue, I will go to the theatre, and the opera, and the ballet. Handsome young men will call for me in their dark blue suits and escort me to the most expensive restaurants, where I will dine on magnificent foods, like roasted duckling with delicate orange sauce, and creamy chocolate pudding, and lovely cherry tarts piled high with whipped cream. And I will never eat another potato as long as I live."

I paused to relish the imaginary taste of the chocolate pudding, and found myself yawning also. "And when I'm tired, at the end of a wonderful day, I will sit in front of a roaring fire in my red velvet chair and I will read and read...and read...

I put my head on Mama's shoulder and I could hear Rachel's even breathing as she slept with her head in Mama's lap. Mama stroked my hair, and as I closed my eyes, she whispered, "Thank you for sharing your splendid dreams. I hope with all my heart that they will come true. Now, sleep my children, there is no telling what awaits us."

CHAPTER VI

As my eyes began to slowly open, I again became aware of where we were. With a sinking feeling in my stomach, I heard the rumble of the train, the cries of the children, and the moaning of the old people who might never survive this ride. My open eyes were greeted with the brightness of a new day as the sunlight tried to force its way through the boxcar siding. A new day in the Ghetto usually brought with it renewed hope for a better life when the War was over. This new day only brought the dread that comes with not knowing how the day will end.

"Mama, I have to pee," whined Rachel as she tried to stretch and found there was no room for such luxuries.

"I know," said Mama, who also squirmed uncomfortably in the choking closeness of a boxcar. "We'll be there soon, Rachel, try to hold on a bit longer. It's so dreadful in here, let's try not to add to the foulness."

"I don't know if I can, Mama," whispered Rachel, who was now embarrassed by the prospect of having a bathroom accident in the middle of the train car.

"Try hard, sweet girl, and think of pleasant things. Can you do that?"

The man was awake. When he heard Mama talk to Rachel, it was his cue to offer some more of his sarcastic, cynical...yet interesting commentary.

"Pleasant things, eh? Now let me see, since this is such an ideal environment for pleasant thoughts. Perhaps, we could all think of pleasant things to eat. How about steamy bowls of hot oatmeal with brown sugar and strawberries? Yes, strawberries would be perfect, with lots and lots of strong, hot coffee."

"Again, the busy-body!" shouted Mama.

"I'm hungry, Mama, very hungry," whined Rachel.

At this point, I couldn't keep still another moment. "You're just full of complaints, aren't you, Rachel? Do you think there is anyone in this car, on this whole train, that is not hungry or does not need to pee. Do you think Mama and I don't need to pee, also? Shall we ask? The pee would probably flow like the Danube. And I dare say, my dear sister, there are many who already have not been able to hold it. So, if you must, just pee and then be still."

"I don't care what you say, I don't care about these people, I don't even know them. I'm hungry and I have to pee. That's all I care about," snapped Rachel.

"Grow up, Rachel," I snapped right back.

With that, Rachel turned away as best she could. She crossed her arms across her chest and stomped her foot. It would have been actually funny...if it weren't so sad.

"Girls, please," said Mama, "I hate this too, everyone does. But we can't change what is happening. We just have to endure it, darlings. We simply have no choice."

And then came the man's voice again. "That's right, no choice! We must endure this sadistic madness. Let us all endure!" And he laughed a laughed that gave me goose-bumps.

"Let us all just sit quietly and allow these maniacs to take our children, to take our parents, to take our lives and, maybe even our souls. Shall we all hold hands and endure this insanity together?"

And then he stopped being sarcastic and got very angry. "What is the matter with all of you? Why do we let this happen to us? I am old, I cannot fight any longer...but so many of you are young, strong. Why do you just sit there and let this happen? If we join together and use our brains and our wits as one, perhaps, just

41

perhaps, we can figure a way out of this. Or at least, die trying. We are allowing them to take us like stupid cows to the slaughter! We even ride in the same box-cars as the cattle. Soon our carcasses will be hanging right along side the dead livestock."

Then Mama was furious. "SHUT UP! SHUT UP, YOU TERRIBLE MAN!! Can't you see the suffering in this moving coffin? We sit here suffocating from the stench of fear and the oppressive heat of a hundred bodies pressed together and you talk to us about fighting? You call us stupid cows because we are forced at gunpoint to submit to this torture? Are you so blind that you cannot hear the pain that your words cause? If we could fight our way out of this, don't you think we would do it?"

And he replied, "No, because we are all afraid. History will remember us as the victims, not the fighters. We have all heard the rumors, only they are not rumors. They are the truth. How many of us will have to die before it will end? The world will know the numbers, only when it is too late."

Mama began to cry, "Please stop, I can't stand this another moment. I will scream if you don't stop."

And he did...because the train came to a screeching halt.

Everyone was very still. It was eerie how quiet the boxcar became. It was as if everyone, including the babies, were holding their collective breaths.

I squeezed forward so I could get a good look out of the siding slats. I will never forget the first thing I saw, as I squinted into the bright morning sun. Flowers! There seemed to be thousands of flowers, and I could only see a short distance. They were the same jewel-colored flowers that we had in our garden before we were forced to move to Warsaw. The same brilliantly

42

colored flowers that Aunt Ada had around her house in Lowicz.

I turned around with difficulty and pushed my way back to Mama and Rachel. "Mama, Mama, there are flowers. Flowers all over, every color, it's beautiful. How can this be a bad place when there are so many flowers? And listen. Do you hear? They are playing for us, the Merry Widow Waltz. It's my favorite, Mama. Isn't it lucky that awful soldier made me bring my violin? Because maybe that's what I will do, maybe I will play my violin to welcome all of the trains, just like they're doing for us. I can't believe this, Mama, we were so worried about coming to this place and there is nothing to worry about, not when they greet us with flowers and music."

"Foolish girl," came the man's voice yet one more time. "Do you really think they are welcoming you to a pleasant place? They are clever, these Nazis. It is their way of deceiving you, and you believe. God help us all."

"What does he mean, Mama? Why would they try to trick us?" I pleaded with Mama, who only shook her head and mumbled, "I don't know, Hanna, I just don't know."

As we stood there, the three of us, holding onto each other and our bags, the large wooden doors were rolled open with an ear-splitting roar. The sunlight was so bright as it filled the boxcar, that we had to cover our eyes. The next second, we heard a loud and angry voice yell, "All right, Jews, get down out of there! Hurry! Hurry!"

When I was able to open my eyes enough to see out of the door, the sight that greeted me made me stand motionless in a near state of shock. Yes, there were flowers, flowers everywhere. But then I remembered, it was November. How was it possible to grow summer flowers in November? When I looked closer, there was something not quite right about these flowers. It was as if they were made out of something artificial. Was that possible? Sitting on the vast lawn in front of where the trains had stopped, were, at least, thirty young women, no older than me. They sat on wooden folding chairs, in front of black music stands, each with a red swastika painted on the front. The girls all wore white blouses, navy blue skirts, and black oxford shoes. And they all had no hair. None of them had hair, not a single one. They all played violins, or violas, and there were two young women playing cellos. None of them smiled, and all of them looked like death. I don't think I've ever seen so many ghastly thin people all sitting in one place. What I soon learned, was that these girls looked well fed, compared to what I was yet to see. I could never before remember being so terrified.

Mama gave a little whimper that I wasn't quite able to decipher, and she pulled us to her as if she needed our warmth on this beautiful, fifty-degree day.

A man came to the door of the car and shoved it hard to open it wide. I looked at his face and what I saw startled me and filled me with dread, both at the same time. This man with dark, soft eyes looked like he should have been on the train with us. He was a Jew, beyond any doubt, but instead, it appeared that he was working for the Nazis in some way. He was dressed in filthy black and white striped pants and a shirt to match, and an old, tattered sweater that had a yellow Star of David sewn on the front. I was very confused.

"Get up, lady," he said in a harsh voice, but there was also a hint of sympathy in his eyes. "Go stand in that line there and throw your bag on the pile with the others."

"What on earth for?" Mama protested. "All of our things are in there."

"Don't make a scene, lady, just do like you're told, otherwise you, for sure, won't need any of that stuff ever again."

"What does he mean by that, Hanna?" whispered Rachel with a great deal of fear in her voice.

"I have no idea, Rachel, except that I'm sure he meant every word. What I don't understand, is why there is a Jew helping the Nazis. It's all so confusing, I'm beginning to think this is really all a bad dream and we'll wake up soon..."

"Stop your chatter, girl. Throw down your cases and get out of that car," the Jewish Nazi helper shouted. I later learned these Jews were called Kapos, and there were many of them.

"I can't," cried Rachel, "I need to have my suitcase!"

On hearing Rachel's protests, a large, angry looking soldier came over to our car and started yelling at Rachel. "Do as you're told, stupid Jew girl. You'll get the damn thing back later, there's no room on the truck. Now get your foul bodies off that train."

"Do as he says, Rachel. It will be fine. Go on now," I urged, not knowing if it would be fine at all.

I saw that Mama was standing over to the side in a line of other women, and I couldn't help but notice that she had tears streaming down her face. My heart was breaking for her.

We did as the soldier ordered and threw down our suitcases, but I held onto my violin case for dear life. I was not about to take the chance that my precious violin would be damaged. Rachel jumped down and I followed, still clutching the violin to my body.

"Now stand in line there. Stand up straight, all of you, so we can see what we have here, and we can designate you," the soldier growled again. I thought he might be an SS officer like the soldier who took us from our home, by the stripes on his uniform.

"What does he mean, 'designate'?" whispered Rachel.

"Now how should I know, Rachel? Does it look like I've been here before?" I know I wasn't being very sympathetic to Rachel's fear, but I had my own fears to worry about and I wasn't exactly in the mood to answer ridiculous questions.

We both went and stood by Mama, she put her arms around both of us and held on tight and we all cried together as we watched the SS officer move down the line. I couldn't believe what he was doing as he briefly spoke to each woman. He appeared to be examining their bodies, looking them all over carefully, and even touching some. The old and very young were almost instantly dismissed and sent to a truck. The others, he lingered over, even appearing to be enjoying himself.

When he finally came to us, all three of us stood frozen, as if we were made of solid ice.

He spoke to Rachel. "How old are you?"

"I'm thirteen, but I'll be fourteen in two months," answered Rachel and she even managed a smile.

"Do you think I care when you will be fourteen, impudent girl?" he replied as he began to feel her body.

Rachel was overcome with embarrassment and tried to push his hands away, but all he did was laugh.

"Do you play an instrument?" he asked, to which Rachel shook her head no.

"Then get on that other truck over there. You have nothing to offer anyone, except a young body that can work. And, who knows, maybe we can find some other things to use you for." He laughed again.

Next, he stopped in front of Mama. "You, you are the mother of these girls?"

46

"Yes, they are my children. I also have..."

"Shut up, woman! Did I ask what else you have? How old are you?"

Mama was shaking now, as much from anger as from fear. "I am forty years old."

"Do you play an instrument?" he asked.

"I used to play the piano, but..."

"We have no pianos here. Go to that truck there with the other old women," he laughed.

If the whole situation hadn't been so horrible, I'm sure I would have laughed just then, because Mama gave him the most deadly look I had ever seen. I am also sure, that if this had been peace-time and this repulsive man had called her an old woman, she probably would have punched him in the nose. I'm very glad she was so scared, because he didn't look like he would have been too understanding about my mother's temper.

Then it was my turn, he spoke into my face and I smelled the beer and the garlic he ate for lunch. He was so close that I could see the pores in his skin and feel his spittle, as he yelled at me.

"Why do you not throw the case on the pile like you were ordered to do?"

"Because this is my violin. I can't take the chance that it might be ruined," I answered as calmly as I could.

"So, it appears we have found, at least, one useful one. How long have you played, and what do you play?" he asked.

"I've studied the violin for five years, and I play Shubert and Chopin and Strauss and..."

"Uh huh. How old are you?"

"I am fifteen, yesterday," I answered.

He laughed again. "So this is not a very nice birthday party...now is it?"

"No, sir," I said as I looked at the ground.

"And polite too, huh. Now let's see if you have other virtues," he laughed as he roughly pulled my coat open. At first he looked me over from head to foot and pulled my arms away from my body so he could look at my breasts. I'm sure I must have turned twelve shades of crimson, and when I glanced over at Mama and Rachel, they had both turned away so they would not have to see my embarrassment.

When I thought he was finally done with me, the indignities only became worse. He snatched the violin case out of my hands, handed it off to the Jewish Nazi helper, and then he turned me around so that my back was toward him. He pulled my body in so close to him that I could feel the gun he wore on a holster around his chest and then he reached around me and cupped my breasts in his big, sweaty, repulsive hands. His let his hands travel down my body until they were holding me around the hips and then he pulled me close into his body, so that I could feel his private parts hard against my back. I was shaking with fear and disgust as he swung me around to face him once again. I gagged, and he laughed.

"This one will do nicely. Ah, I see a fire in your eyes, little Jew girl. That is the only decent thing about you filthy swine, you have a fire that I love to put out." He laughed loudly yet again and licked his lips. And I did all I could do not to vomit on his shoes.

"Take her to building eleven," he threw orders to the Jew. "And when they cut her hair, save it for me. I have a passion for red hair." He laughed still again and I knew I'd begin screaming if he didn't stop.

"I have just given you a present, girl. I will expect your 'thank yous' later. Happy Birthday, Jew."

As the Kapo took my arm and handed my violin back to me, I heard Rachel's voice and turned. "I have to go with my Mother," she shouted, as she broke from the line and started running toward Mama. "I have to...please!" She didn't get but a few steps, when the Kapo let go of my arm and headed toward Rachel.

"Stop it, little girl, don't be foolish. They will kill you," he whispered, loud enough for me to hear.

"I don't care, I don't care. I would rather die than get touched by these wicked men. I want to be with my Mama!" Rachel shouted as she broke free again. This time, the SS officer caught her by the back of her coat.

"GRAB HER AND HOLD HER, DAMN YOU!" he shouted at the Kapo, who grabbed Rachel around the waist as she continued to scream and kick.

"Little girl, stop this...stop this. Don't you know that you are being spared?"

"I DON'T CARE! I want to be with my Mama!"

My eyes flew back and forth between the two...from Rachel to Mama and back again. Finally, Mama could keep still no longer and she ran to Rachel's side. "No, please, Rachel, my child. Please do as they say."

And then she turned her anger toward the Kapo. "Leave her alone, you! Take your dirty, traitor hands off her. You people are crazy! How can you treat human beings like this? And you, you are a Jew, for God's sake! How can you do such things? You turn against your own people for a few scraps of bread? Where is your God? Where is your humanity? You think they will let you live because you help them? You are as big a fool as you are detestable. They will not let you live, they will not want to leave any witnesses to this. The man on the train was right, he was right..."

49

With that, the SS officer rose to his full height and swung his arm with such force, that when his hand found Mama's face it knocked her to the ground. When she looked up, her nose was bloodied, and she had the dirt from the ash-covered ground all over her beautiful face.

The officer grabbed her by the hair and lifted her to her feet shouting, "QUIET! Damn you, Jew dog! Damn you all!"

A terrible thing happened then.

Rachel began crying uncontrollably and she began to scream, "MAMA...MAMA...MAMA..." over and over and over, until in her panic and hysteria, she wet herself. When she realized what she had done, she began to moan and it was a sound I will never forget. It was the sound of the wind howling past the grave-stones in a cemetery, it was as if a dead child had risen from the grave and cried out its fury at having been cheated out of life. I don't know what Rachel's mind was telling her at that moment, and I would never be able to find out, but the anguish I heard was so filled with rage and fear that I had to cover my ears as the tears poured from my eyes.

When I looked up again, I saw Mama's face all contorted with hatred as she began to shout at the Jew and the SS officer.

"You crazy, evil bastards! These are innocent children. What would you do if you saw your own children treated with such cruelty? You are not human! You are not! You are devils and I hope you all rot in Hell for your sins!"

But before she could say more, the SS officer struck her across the face again, this time causing her eye to swell almost instantly, which brought more cries of outrage from Rachel.

50

"Mama...Mama! Please don't hit her again, please," I pleaded with the SS officer. He only turned to me, as he grabbed Rachel by the arm. And he shouted, "You, you shut your mouth, or you will soon join these two. And you," he said to Rachel, "you want to be with your Mama? Go...go be with your Mama."

He called to a soldier standing at the head of the line, "Take them away from me!" And then, he took out a spotlessly clean, white handkerchief and wiped his sweating face and neck.

Mama made one last break from the line, and ran up to me. She grabbed me to her in a desperate hug, and let go only long enough to touch my face, look into my eyes and whisper, "It will be all right, sweet Hanna, it will be fine. I will see you soon, when they have done whatever it is they have to do, I will see you again."

"Please, don't cry, Mama, I love you so," I whispered back. And then she covered my face with kisses, until the SS officer saw what she was doing.

He ran over, grabbed her by the hair again, and at the same time drew his pistol. He said only two words, "Good-bye Jew." Then he shot my mother in the head.

Miriam Berkenski, that beautiful, devoted woman who lived only to love her family, crumpled like a broken doll at my feet and the only blessing was that she left this world before she ever hit the ground.

I fell to my knees and held her in my arms for only a second, for when I looked up, the officer was pointing the gun at me. "Get up, I will not kill you unless you force me too, like your half-witted mother. You are too interesting to me, I need you...for several things." He laughed again over the body of my mother and for the second time in five minutes, I wanted to vomit at his feet.

I stood up with Mama's blood all over my arms, and when I looked over to find Rachel, she was gone. Her line had been loaded into the truck and they were pulling away from the train. I never knew what she saw that day...and I never saw her again.

CHAPTER VII

The next three years were a nightmare of pain. The pain of loss, the pain of constant hunger, the pain of helplessness, the pain of hopelessness, the pain of physical and mental abuse, and the pain of guilt. They were the pains that I woke with each morning and went to sleep with each night. They never left me. They became my constant companions, and in a way, my friends; because they reminded me I was still alive.

On the day my Mama died and Rachel disappeared, I was taken to a low, wooden building with twenty other young women. Some were older than I, but most were around my age. And there was one girl in particular.

When we were lined up inside the building, she stood next to me and took my hand. I looked at her and she smiled a tiny smile that said to me, "We will help each other." For the next three years, we did. In that one moment, we became sisters, and if it were not for our bond, I am sure neither Silva Braunstein nor I would have left that awful place with our minds intact.

Silva was also from Warsaw, I was to find out. The Ghetto, being as large as it was, meant that people on the east side, probably never knew the people on the west side. Silva was sixteen and very plump on that first day at Auschwitz. This was a fact she attributed to her father's ability to smuggle butter, and sausages, and chocolate creams into the Ghetto at night. He had owned a large grocery in Warsaw and one of his non-Jewish vendors had been his friend since childhood.

Within a very short time, though, Silva was no longer plump. That was a condition she was not altogether sad about, although she never stopped talking about how much she missed the chocolate creams. Some days, we would amuse and torture ourselves by planning the perfect, imaginary feast. I particularly liked the meat and fresh vegetable fantasies. Silva, of course, most enjoyed the desserts.

"Do you know, Hanna, that in Austria they have pastries with every meal?" she told me one day. "Yes, it's very true. I know this because my cousin Bella lives there. Before the War, when we didn't have to live in that miserable apartment, she used to come for holiday every summer. And do you know what she would bring? Chocolate coconut bars, and lemon tarts, and eclairs filled with vanilla custard. Can you imagine people eating such sweets every day? She said they have these wonderful cinnamon buns with white icing for breakfast, and chocolate cookies with pecans for lunch, and blueberry scones with clotted cream and strawberry jam for tea, and for dinner...Napoleons as high as a man's nose. Of course, I don't exactly believe the Napoleons were that high, but what a wonderful possibility. Don't you think?"

"Silva, if we ate pastries like that every day, we would be as large as a dirigible and with rotten teeth besides."

"Well," she said very seriously, "have you ever seen the Austrians?" We looked at each other for just a second and then burst out laughing. It was our talks about nonsense that helped to keep my spirit alive when all around me was the smell of death.

And so as we stood in line, we were told about our various jobs while we were in the camp, and also about the penalties for disobeying orders. If there was any tiny cell in our bodies that wasn't petrified with fear already, the talk about penalties took care of that cell.

Silva was to play violin, the same as me, but when she wasn't playing, she was to work in the Commandant's laundry. Silva's job seemed like a vacation in Vienna, filled with her beloved pastries, compared to what they had in store for me.

Apparently, the SS officer at the train, who I later found out, was named Fredrick Gotmann, had taken a fancy to my red hair and ample bosom, and ordered that I be sent to him almost every night. Some nights, he would sit, and drink cognac, and tell me about his love of Germany and the Fuehrer.

"This is the most beautiful country on the face of the Earth," he would croon. "The mountains, the trees, the feeling of brotherhood among the pure. The Fuehrer is right you know, I have known this for a long time. We can only be great if we are pure. And then, when we have selected out the dirty froth, my little Jew girl, then we will rule the universe."

On those nights he was fairly gentle with me.

Other nights he would pace, and drink beer, smoke ugly cigars, and tell me about his loathing of Adolf Hitler and the entire Third Reich.

"Hitler is crazy," he would shout. "I know this for a fact because I spent time with him in Munich. The man is mad, stark raving mad. Oh, don't get me wrong, I agree that we need to rid Europe of the contaminants, but him and his band of misfits are trying to do this neatly. It can't be done neatly. Shoot them all, bury them deep and be done. Instead, they play games, waste my time. Idiots!"

On those nights, he treated me roughly and sent me away crying.

And, on still other nights, he would drink straight whisky, and tell me how much he hated the Jews for starting the War in the first place.

"Pigs! Filthy money-grabbing, liars," he would whisper. "Your people, they are the ones responsible for this. They are the cause of their own suffering. They foul the very ground they walk on, and killing them is a blessing and a service to the rest of humanity."

On those nights, he would force me to fulfill his most repulsive fantasies and when he finally allowed me to leave, I could barely walk back to building eleven.

At first, I was filled with shame, and self-loathing, and my young body ached most of the time from his brutal treatment.

Even on the days when he was sober, I was still nursing bruises and torn private parts, so that I never had a chance to recover from one time to the next. Physical pain became a constant. Rape was a way of life.

As the months became years though, my body and mind became numb to his words, and to his touch. I think as time went on, he became fond of my visits, because it gave him a chance to act out his aggressions against the Jews. I was the representation of everything he hated about the War. I was the symbol for what he would like to do to every Jew in the world.

There were times when he would smile, and joke, and tell me stories from his childhood and his desires for a life of beauty and peace after the War ended - all of the things that intimate partners should share, he shared with me. I never offered even my name. When I wouldn't tell him, he found out from the list which came with our train. The funny thing is, in all three years that I was to spend servicing this creature, he never used my name once. He simply called me, 'Jew girl'.

The only thing that kept me sane, was to lie beside Silva at night and plan his gruesome and torturous death. That, unfortunately, was one flight of fancy I would never be able to carry out. But, it gave me great solace to think that some day, some how, I might.

The other job I was given during the days when I was not playing my violin, was something I can hardly describe without beginning to shake. I will tell that part later.

#####

On that fifty degree day of our arrival, they forced us to strip naked, and they marched us out to shower stalls in the yard next to the building, where they made us soap and rinse ourselves in freezing cold water. They then marched us back into the building, had us all share two towels, and gave us each an ugly, shapeless, black and white striped dress, to wear with only the undergarments we had worn before. They also handed each of us a navy blue skirt, and a plain white blouse, just like the women's string ensemble had worn earlier. This was to be my "concert" uniform, the clothes I would wear whenever I played to greet the trains arriving at the Auschwitz Concentration Camp train station.

After dressing, they took us one by one to a small table. When it was my turn, a very young soldier sat me in a wooden chair. He didn't look much older than Sammy. There was a woman wearing rubber surgical gloves, who didn't smile or even acknowledge my presence. While the soldier held my arm to the table with the soft, sensitive side turned up, the woman tattooed five numbers and one letter on my arm...A15311. This was a practice used at all of the Nazi concentration camps, and was used as a means of identifying the prisoners. The ones that were killed upon arrival, had no need for tattoos.

And then, of course, they cut off my hair.

I thank God every day for giving me the talent to pull a bow across four strings. Because, between my daily rehearsals, my "concert" schedule, and my nights devoted to detesting one human with a passion so great,

57

that at times I thought I could destroy the world with my burning hatred. I had only enough time left for my "other" job...and for sleep.

CHAPTER VIII

Time went by in a blur of sadness, and I often thought of my mother and sister. I knew, of course, that Mama was dead, and I was fairly sure that Rachel was also, because I never saw her again, not even once, in the entire three years. Although a tiny part of my heart still hoped that she was working in a kitchen somewhere in the camp, or perhaps that she had been transferred to another camp, my brain told me that wasn't so. I had seen too many trains come into the station, too many helpless people marched away in long lines, to hope she had survived. As for my father and Sammy and Esther, my mind refused to even take me on that journey.

And so, every day was just like the last, and exactly like the next. Each week blended with the week before and one month became indistinguishable from the one following.

The only way we were able to gauge the passage of time was to notice the changing seasons. Winters were the worst, because there was ice everywhere, on everything, all of the time. And we still had to go about our daily routines and perform our "concerts" in the snow and freezing winds with nothing but moth eaten sweaters on our backs.

I had told Mama, on the train, that I would never again eat another potato if it possibly could be avoided. But, here I was consuming potato soup daily, which was more often than not, made from rotten and moldy spuds. To go along with the soup, they fed us stale bread in large chunks that were almost impossible to chew and for us, the performers, an occasional helping of salt pork to keep us strong. It was, of course, a joke we could not even laugh at, and many of us learned to beg God's forgiveness for eating swine, because we knew he would understand...under the circumstances.

"I can't eat this, Silva, it's a sin," I said on the first night they delivered the pork to our building. "This goes against everything I've been taught my whole life."

"Is that so?" she whispered, so the others could not hear. "And were you not taught that it's a sin to murder, and rape, and deceive? You live with those sins every day of your life in this hellhole. That disgusting Nazi who takes you for his pleasure every night, is that not a sin? The trains that bring the Jews by the hundreds for the sole purpose of murdering innocent people, is that not a sin? The fact that we sit and play a waltz as they are marched to their deaths, is that not a sin too?"

"But those are the sins of the Nazis, not the sins of the Jews," I protested.

"Then let the demons have one more. They starve us to death and only offer us pig meat when they know it is against our laws and our faith to eat it. I, for one, will not let them get away with yet another sin against us. I will fight with the only weapon I have left to use against them. I will survive this, Hanna! I will walk out of here strong enough to tell the world what they did. And if it takes eating this meat to do that, then so be it."

Many of the women chose not to partake. I chose to follow Silva and to live. And, after the first few times of choking down the alien flesh, I finally convinced myself that God had given his approval, just this once. I actually began to look forward to the salt pork as a welcome change from the rotten potato soup.

#####

In the mornings, after we lined up for roll call and eaten our ration of soup and bread, we were made to practice together for two hours. We were given sheet music on the first day, and after several weeks of work, the women in building eleven were actually quite good.

I am sure, and history will bear me out, that the Germans in 1941 were a cultured people. Even the Nazis, during peacetime, no doubt enjoyed the Arts from time to time, and entertained interests other than murder. But these Nazis who ran Auschwitz, well, let's just say that they didn't have very much imagination.

Our classical repertoire consisted of only two pieces, which we played over, and over, and over again. The Tales of Hoffman, and The Merry Widow Waltz, were the mellow sounds that greeted the doomed each day. I, of course, knew The Merry Widow Waltz from before, so it was a bit easier for me to learn. It's funny to think that at one time, The Merry Widow was actually my favorite of all the lovely Viennese waltzes. I soon learned to detest the very sound of it.

#####

Building eleven had an interesting assortment of women. All were good-looking girls still in their late teens and early twenties. They came from all over Europe, and some spoke languages which others of us could not understand. The thing that bonded us and allowed us to communicate, if even superficially, was that we were all Jews and we all spoke at least some Yiddish.

There was this one young woman, I remember, who was about twenty-years-old. She came to building eleven about a month after Silva and I arrived. Her name was Seena Hirschberg, and she was from Germany. Her family had managed to escape to Holland with hundreds of other Jews, but before they could be taken

61

to a safe haven, they were captured and transported to Auschwitz.

The most interesting thing about Seena, was that somehow she had managed to be put into the women's string orchestra, and she couldn't play a note. It wasn't that she even played poorly, she had literally never held a violin in her life. Apparently, one of the other officers took a fancy to her rather voluptuous body, and decided it would be worth sparing her, if we could teach her to play. We tried, oh, how we tried to teach Seena to play. But, it became evident after a very short time that she was not only lacking in talent, but also lacking in brains.

"I can't do this, Hanna," whined Seena one morning when we were supposed to be practicing. "I keep trying to make this silly stick slide nicely across these strings, and all I get is the sound of a sick alley-cat."

"Try spitting in your hand, Seena, and then run your bow through the saliva," said one of the other girls. All of the women in the room began to laugh so loudly, that it brought one of the guards running with his pistol drawn.

"What is going on in here?" shouted the guard.

We immediately stopped laughing and began to practice again, no one daring to meet his eyes. "That's better," he growled, "and just keep it that way. You think you are privileged, huh? You are only lucky! Nothing more. One more outburst from you hyenas and I may be forced to have a little accident with my pistol. And wouldn't that be a shame, huh?" Then he turned and left the building, mumbling something about "stupid Jewish cows". When he was well out of ear-shot, we all put our hands to our mouths and laughed like silly school-girls until our bodies ached. It felt wonderful to laugh. The only one who didn't laugh was poor Seena Hirschberg.

Seena, fortunately, managed to stay alive. We assumed her sexual talents were more important to the right people than her lack of talent with the strings.

We looked out for each other and I can honestly say, as awful as those years were, they were in some strange ways, rewarding. Together we all shared the same terrible experiences. We all grieved for our lost loved ones, we all shared the horrors we were forced to witness during the 'other' parts of our days, we all cried bitter tears together, and we all held tight to each other in the cold nights.

CHAPTER IX

And that brings us to my 'other' job.

On some days I played the music of the Masters, even if it was only two pieces. And on those days, I would sit with the others on the grassy hill, surrounded by real flowers in the spring, summer, and fall, and by ugly, fake flowers in the winter. The Nazis spared no expense to create their illusion. They commissioned the finest artificial flowers in the world to complete their clever fraud. To me, however, they were hideous reminders of the things they had taken away from us. The beauty of the real world, the freedom to enjoy nature without the bonds of barbed wire, and the trickery they employed to take it all away.

We would sit, and play, and watch the trains pull in. I saw the hundreds of lost, defeated, hopeless people, as they spilled out of the wooden cattle cars. Some days I thought it was as if the huge steam engine was regurgitating its last meal, one which didn't sit right on its insides.

Not just the Jews, but the Catholics, the Gypsies, the homosexuals, the mentally ill, the physically disabled, and the Blacks, and on, and on, and on... So many children too, frightened and hungry, so many babies, unaware of their fates, so many elderly, all too aware of theirs. I saw these people day after day, as I played a lovely little waltz to welcome them to their destruction. All of the faces began to look the same. All of the eyes became one pair of terrified eyes.

When I stopped playing, I ate my salt pork, and changed back into my ragged striped dress, and went to work in the death house.

It was a huge, ominous, red brick building that housed, among other things, the clinics where gruesome experiments were being conducted daily by the Nazi Dr. Frankensteins. These experiments were conducted on human guinea pigs, who were almost always the sick, the disabled, or the young. They ranged from such frightful procedures as cutting off various body parts and attaching them to other parts of the victim's body, to trying out various methods of causing death on different types of people, and watching to see how long it took them to die. Perhaps the Nazis were creative after all.

Also contained within those gloomy walls, were the gas chambers and the crematoria.

My job was to help the men who prepared the gas chambers to receive the next batch of unsuspecting victims.

These same men, who I later found out were called Sonderkommandos, were also responsible for removing the bodies, carrying them to the ovens, and then disposing of the ashes afterward. The thing that made these men different from the SS, was that they were all inmates, all fellow prisoners at Auschwitz. They were Jews and non-Jews alike, who were enlisted by the SS to do the dirtiest of the dirty work, and then they were often killed so they could not bear witness to the slaughter. It again showed the cleverness of the Nazis.

Eventually though, as happened in 1943 and 1944, the camp became so busy, that they ordered some of us sturdier women to help with the death house "chores". The Sonderkommando never spoke to us, they never even looked at us, perhaps out of shame, or perhaps out of fear that if they disobeyed the orders to never mingle with the other prisoners, they would be shot on the spot.

They were beaten-down, angry men, who were forced to do some of the most un-Godly tasks any human could imagine. And because of this, some of the weaker spirits soon succumbed to the horrors of their jobs and took their own lives. I saw one man, throw himself into the gas chamber, only seconds before the doors were slammed and sealed. Another, who on discovering that one of the bodies he was about to feed into the oven, was his own cousin, threw himself into the fire instead of facing that deed.

I was assigned to help with groups of women who were about to be exterminated. I would have to stand aside as they undressed, and then I would collect their clothing and jewelry, separating each piece by value.

Once undressed, the women would be lined up and marched into, what they were told were "the showers", as I made sure they entered the chamber in an orderly manner. Afterwards, I would leave to help another group, as the Sonderkommandos began to remove the bodies and clean out the chamber.

This is not a subject I care to linger over, so I will tell one story of what happened on my first day in that place, a day they made me watch everything, so I would know what awaited me if I mentioned any of it to anyone. I knew on that day my fate was probably sealed, and that it was only a matter of time before I too, became a victim. Ironically, my hated visits to Fredrik Gotmann, were probably the only things that were allowing me to live. But what I saw and heard that day, has haunted my dreams ever since.

#####

There was a woman and her young daughter. The child reminded me very much of my sister, Rachel, but perhaps a little younger. I was to help them and the

66

others disrobe, and so I was able to over-hear their conversations.

There were also two of the Sonderkommandos watching. One of them shouted, "Take off your clothes quickly and put them all in that pile over there," as he pointed to an already huge mountain of female clothing that I was trying to sort. "And if you have any jewelry take it off and place it on the table."

I remember glancing at the table and being astounded at the collection of gold and gems that lay there as if on display at the museum in Warsaw. Later, I would be instructed on how to determine the valuable pieces from the paste.

"But why do we need to remove everything?" asked the woman.

"Because, you stupid cow, you are going to the showers," said the man. "You can't shower with your clothes on, now can you?"

I had heard rumors before about what went on in this building, but this was the first time I had actually seen it with my own eyes. Up to this point, I still didn't believe that the Nazis would really do what I had heard.

"I don't want to take my clothes off, Mama, it's cold in here," said the child.

"You must," said the woman. "Don't think about what you're doing. Just look at my face and we will talk."

"I'll try, Mama."

"Good, that's good. Now, what would you like to talk about?"

"Tell me about Father. I wonder where he is," said the girl.

And then she began. "Your father is the love of my life, and I am sure he is somewhere safe. I don't think you really know your father very well, my darling, you're still so young. But, he is the kindest man I have ever known, gentle, compassionate, and generous to a fault. Let me tell you a story."

And as they continued to undress, I listened in on her story.

"When we were much younger," the woman said, "before you blessed our lives, your father began teaching at the University."

I listened even harder now, because I wondered if it was the same university where my own Papa had taught, before the War. Maybe they even knew each other.

"He was very much loved by his students," she continued. "They used to come to the house all the time for long discussions about music and politics...and my pickled beef. That was in the days when even if you were poor you could still afford a piece of meat to share. Often they would confide in him about private matters. He was much more to them than a teacher, he was a friend."

At that point, it was all I could do to contain myself from interrupting. It was as if my own mother and sister were standing in front of me, unclothed and telling the story of my family. I wanted so badly to reach out and hold them, and tell them that my Papa, too, had taught at a University. That he too, had befriended his students and gave them food and comfort, I wanted to tell them how sorry I was. And then I was overcome with guilt at being spared, while this nameless mother and daughter were being prepared to die.

The tears began to cover my cheeks as she continued her story.

"Well, one day," she said, "he received a letter from a young man, whom he had instructed only a year before, and who had been to our home several times. He told

68

your father of his troubles and of his need for money. Your good-hearted father sat right down and answered his letter. Then he went to our money-box, took a whole week's grocery money, and put it in the envelope with the letter. He said, 'Rivka, please understand, I have to do this.' So I shook my head okay, because I trusted your father to know what was the right thing to do."

"What did you do for a week without grocery money?" asked the girl.

"Well, your father shoveled manure in Mr. Schultz's stable every day after school for two weeks to make up the difference."

In spite of their terrible situation, the mother, named Rivka, and her child started to giggle, and I couldn't help but giggle right along with them. I covered my mouth with both hands and pretended to cough, so one of the men would not turn his acid tongue, or his fists, on me.

The woman and child were silent for a few moments as they finished undressing. Then they clung to each other, perhaps from the cold, perhaps out of the shame of nakedness, or perhaps out of sheer terror at what would happen next.

As I stood back, I watched them waiting in line with, what seemed to be several hundred other women. I couldn't help wonder where their men were taken.

"We're going to die now, Mama, aren't we?" said the child, so innocently that it instantly brought tears again to my eyes. "Just like the rumors we heard on the train?"

"Yes, my love, I think maybe we are," said the woman.

And then this child who was younger than my own sister, said something that made me sob out loud. For-

69

tunately for me that day, the death house was extremely busy, and so the men again overlooked me.

"I'm not so afraid to die, Mama, not like I thought I'd be," said the child. "This seems almost like a bad dream, and I'll wake up soon. But if it's not, Mama, then I'll be sad to leave this world without ever knowing a great love like you had with Father."

"Oh my dear child, I am so, so sorry. For in this life, you will only know my love, and that will have to do. But please understand, my daughter, that no one could ever love you more." And then she kissed the child's face, and held her close, and they both began to cry.

If only there was something I could have done, if only...if only... At that moment, the guilt became so huge and heavy, that I was hardly able to stand. I was alive because I could play. That which separated the living from the dead was only a violin string.

Then I heard an awful sound. It was the sound of the huge steel doors being slid open, followed by the voice of an SS officer, who had just arrived on the scene, apparently to make it all official.

"All right, through that door now, all of you into the showers. Hurry, hurry, move along, move along..."

I heard the sliding door close and the unmistakable sound of the door seal being fixed in place. What followed were the worst sounds I had ever heard or would ever hear again. It was the heart-breaking cries, and moans, and prayers, of the desperate, helpless, frightened victims.

There was a small window in the door, and I positioned myself so I was able to barely see into the 'shower'.

"We are ready, Sergeant Moll," announced the SS officer into a telephone which rested on a shelf to the side of the door. I have since learned, that Sergeant Moll was the executioner at Aucshwitz.

He spoke so loudly at the other end of the phone, that I could make out "Na, gib ihmen schon zu fressen!" he said, and then he laughed.

It is almost unthinkable, that as he put hundreds of Jews to death in one room, at the same time, he would say something as inhuman as, "Now give them something to chew on."

The next sound I heard, was the hissing of the chemicals being pumped into the death chamber. And, what I saw through the little window in the steel door was the face of a woman trying to escape from the inescapable. That face torments me to this day, as do the prayers I heard being screamed up to Heaven.

"Shema yisrael adonai elohaynu adonai echad. Hear O Israel, the Lord our God, the Lord is One."

These were the final words on the lips of the Jews...six million times.

CHAPTER XI

The real work began when the steel doors were opened again. For there, on the floor of that hideous death chamber, lay the remains of human beings, the vessels of several hundred souls.

Since, as I said before, this was my first day, I had to experience everything. So along with others like myself, we were made to remove the bodies, place them on carts that were pulled by the Sonderkommando men, and take them to the other side of the building, which housed the crematoria. Once there, we were to watch as they took the bodies from the carts and disposed of them in the ovens. The most horrifying part, if there could be one part more deplorable than another, was that some of the victims were not yet dead.

Those moments have never left my mind, and much later when I heard about the suicides of the Sonderkommandos, I understood.

And that is all I have to say about that.

The days became weeks and the weeks became months and the months became years. The sameness was somehow comforting. The outrage at being used by the Nazi was replaced with boredom. The boredom of listening to the insanity that came from his lips, the boredom of physical acts that were never connected to reality. They became mechanical and monotonous. They were a way for me to get a cup of tea and a piece of soft bread.

Then there was the sameness of the music. It became so familiar, I was able to close my eyes and rest while my fingers worked independently of my brain.

There was the sameness of Sergeant Moll and his obscene orders to begin the executions. I knew what was coming and so, I knew what I must to do in order to live, and I knew the dead could not judge me, because they all would have done what I did in order to survive.

With all of this sameness, one day melted into the next, and each night became a journey through my imagination. Some nights I dreamt of lovely cottages by a lake, picking flowers with Mama, and sharing a scone and strawberry jam with Rachel.

On other nights, I dreamt of pits of fire, and screaming children, and monstrous-sized men who hid behind barren trees and waited for me to walk by. The ends of my nightmares were always different, and some nights there were no ends, because I would wake up screaming.

I was not alone. Recalling our nightmares, became a favorite pastime in building eleven. Trying to see whose dream was the most gruesome.

Most of the time, the dreams came and went and I would be hard-pressed to remember them by the next afternoon. But, on a Sunday night in October of 1944, I had a dream that I never forget. The reason I know the date so well, is because it was one month before the gassing stopped at Auschwitz.

#####

In the beginning of my dream, I am standing on a large rock in the dead of night. Everything around me is pitch black, except for the sky, which is lit by a full moon and a billion twinkling stars.

Down below me, I see a bedroom and all that illuminates the room is a small bedside lamp. There is a window which looks out on the black, moonlit night, and next to the window is a phono-

73

graph. There is a man standing with his back to me, so I cannot see his face. He wears the uniform of the Nazi party. He appears to be putting a record on the phonograph and then I hear "The Merry Widow Waltz" played by all strings. As the music plays, the man listens and appears to be lost in the melody. He paces for a few moments, stands with his hands clasped behind his back, and then slowly turns to face me. It is Adolf Hitler.

I watch as he walks to the bed, removes his jacket and meticulously places it at the foot of the bed. He then removes his tie, folds it up, and places it in the pocket of his jacket. He rolls up his sleeves and opens the neck of his shirt. He never looks up at me once, but somehow I know he is aware of my presence as he sits on the edge of the bed. Next, he removes his shoes and places them neatly under the bed.

What he does now surprises me, for he opens the drawer of the night table and removes a pistol, which he places on top of the table within easy reach of the bed. He adjusts the pillows and lays back against them as he closes his eyes and continues listening to the music.

I look around me, and in the moonlight I see the silhouettes of people standing in the night. They are in poses of distress, and pleading, and pain. Each one stands alone.

I begin to descend from my hill, only to find that these people are also standing on hills, and I'm confused. I become aware that there is a low ground fog all about me and only the moon to light my way.

"I can't find my way, it all looks the same," I call out to no one and to everyone. "The buildings are all the same, but what is this filthy place? Dirty wooden barracks, running with stench. And these people, so unkempt, so sullen, so thin...especially the children. Why do you keep your children in such squalor? Why do they do this to you?"

In the darkness, I hear an answer I wasn't expecting. "They do this because they can," comes the soft voice of an old and tired man.

74

"Who is that speaking to me?" I call back through the night. There is only silence, so I call again. "What happens if I can't find my way? Can you help me? I'm looking for my home and I don't know which way to go."

Before an answer can come to me, I hear the roar of an airplane engine in the dark sky above. I look up in horror and see the plane has no bottom. I can see into the depths of its belly and all I see is fire.

"Do you see that? Do you see the fire? It's so clear, the fire and the bombs. If they fall, we all will die! Can't you help me, can't you...?"

Then I see Mama. Finally, finally I've found her. She is standing on another hill and she is dressed all in white, like a shroud, like an angel in a shroud.

"Hanna, oh, Hanna, my darling child, come to me," calls Mama, her voice floating off on a gentle breeze. She holds her arms out to me, but as I climb the hill and try to come into her arms, she moves away.

"Mama, I'm so lost. Can you help me? You are the only one I can trust. I need to go home, Mama, can you come with me?"

"Yes, you need to go home, my dear child, but I cannot go with you," whispers Mama.

"I don't understand. I thought you would always be with me. How can I find my way alone?"

"You are never alone, Hanna. As long as you trust yourself, you are never alone. Go see the others and they will tell you."

I wipe the tears from my eyes and walk down the hill. I look around and see an old man, bent from years of hard labor, standing on another hill. He wears an old, black coat, and a battered, old Fedora. He smiles as I approach and holds his hands out to me.

I stand at the bottom of his hill and look up into his sad eyes. "Why are you here, old man?" I ask.

"I am waiting to die. And you?" he replies.

"I am trying to find my way home."

"Yes, I would also like to go home," he says.

"Then maybe we can go together, we will help each other," I say.

"Ah, yes, that would be nice, but I am waiting to die, you see. I would die soon anyway, you know. I am old. But he has made it so the natural order is disobeyed." And he points to the figure of Adolf Hitler who lies in the bed. "He brought me to this place, this hell pit in the middle of the forest. He brought me here to die among the beauty of the sightless trees, and the joy of the bird's song, and the playful scamper of the little animals. Is this a place to make people die, to shoot us as if we were livestock? That is why I can't go home." And then he laughs and cries, both at the same time.

"Who are you?" I asked.

"I am Joseph Schenkel. I want you should remember my face, little girl. When I was still living in my home with clean white sheets on my bed and warm egg bread on my table at the Sabbath, I heard about this evil man, and how he takes young beautiful boys from their Mamas and poisons their minds so they will kill for him. I was told he was a monster, not a human person." He points to the sleeping Hitler down below again, and then continues. "I said to my Rayzel, 'How can a flesh and blood man be so filled with hate that he would do this to people who don't hurt anyone. What makes a man punish so many for his own bitterness?" And do you know what she said, my Rayzel? She said to me, 'He is only lost, Joseph, he is so very lost in his world of anger and bitterness, that no one will escape his fury as long as he is allowed to live.' So, I want you to take a good look at me, my little friend. Do you see my eyes filled with sadness and grief? Do you see my mouth as it says a last prayer? Do you see my ears as they listen to the last gasps of life from my wife and my children? I want you should remember, because my face is that of a Jew. I want you to go home and tell them what you saw."

"I'm sorry, Mr. Schenkel, I'm so very sorry," I whisper as I turn to continue my search. I look around and only see a shooting

76

star, and then I hear another voice coming from another hill. I run in that direction, calling, "Can you tell me the time?"

"There is no time here, Hanna. Can't you see that?" says a woman as thin as a reed blowing in the wind. Her eyes are sunken and she has no hair. I recognize the striped dress, because I wear one just like it.

"There has to be time, there always has to be time," I say, and I am confused again.

"Have it your way," she replies. "If you were me instead of you, you would know there is no time here. There are no such things as seconds or minutes or hours or days, there is only the endless stretch of nothingness, the unbearable void of hopelessness that must be endured. What else do you want to know?"

"How do you know my name?" I ask the woman.

"Because I know you, you are just like my daughter. Only you are not silent."

"No, no I'm not silent. But I don't understand," I say. "But I really must go, because I'm late, because I have been searching all over for my home, and if I don't get there soon..."

"I am so sorry I cannot help you, but I've been assigned to the kitchen," she says.

"Do you get the scraps?" I ask with a bit of envy in my voice and for the moment forget my need to run off.

"Some. I cook for the Commandant, he eats rather well," she tells me. "And...he touches us."

"There are others?"

"Yes, there are others. My daughter, she is only seventeen, like you. He thinks she is beautiful, and he thinks he can touch her. When we lived in Berlin, Brauna was the prettiest girl in the whole Jewish quarter. All of the young boys would follow her home. She wore satin ribbons in her hair which looked like spun gold. Then we had to hide, and she cried all day and all night." She was silent for a few moments and then continued. "And then they found us, and those filthy devils stole her innocence. Do you understand?"

77

I nod and listen.

"In front of my eyes they take her, as she screams for mercy. And then, she stopped. She stopped her screaming. And to this day, she is still silent. She serves the soup, and she serves the vermin each night on their clean sheets. And she is silent. And when they are finished with her, and finally decide to end her misery, she will probably still be silent as the gun is placed to her forehead."

"How do you know they will kill her?" I asked.

"Because I pray for it!" she answers in anger and frustration. "If they let her live, she will walk the Earth until she is old, without a soul. And so, my friend, Hanna, I want you to take a good look at me. I want you to remember, because my face is that of a Jew. I want you to go home and tell them what you saw. Because you are not silent, you have a voice."

We stare at each other for a long time and then I turn and walk back down the hill as I hear the woman call out to me, "You better hurry."

"Mama, Mama, are you here?" I call into the darkness. "I need you to help me!"

"I can help you, Hanna," comes a child's voice from out of the mist.

I twirl around in both directions and I see nothing. "Esther is that you?" I whisper, not knowing why I'm whispering, but it seems so appropriate.

"I'm here, Hanna," she answers as she steps out of the mist and takes my hand. She is dressed in her pajamas, the ones she wore on the day we left, and her little blue coat. She is carrying an old and battered teddy bear, the same one Papa bought for me when I was a child.

"It's me, Esther."

"Why have you been hiding from me, Esther?" I ask.

"So you can't find me, silly," she replies.

"It's not time to play games now, Esther, we need to find our way home."

78

"I know the way, come with me, Hanna," she says as she pulls me toward the sleeping man in the bed down below.

"We can't go there, Esther, it's not safe," I warn, but she pulls me over to the bed and we stand staring at the man.

Slowly, he opens his eyes and looks at Esther, but not at me. "You look frightened, little girl. You are so small, do you think I would hurt you?" the man who looks like Adolf Hitler asks.

"Yes," she answers.

"Are you a Jew?" he asks.

"A what?"

"A Jew. Are you a Jew? Where is your star? It should be sewed on your coat," he says as he sits up and hangs his legs over the side of the bed.

"Mama didn't give me a star on my coat. I would like a star. Stars are sparkly and beautiful. Do you have a star on your coat, Mister?" she asks.

"Of course not. Do you know who I am?"

Esther lets go of my hand and turns away, she looks around for a second and then says, "Come on, Hanna, I don't like it here." And she walks off into the mist. "I need to find Mama, Hanna. Maybe she will give me a star on my coat."

I turn and go to Esther and take her hand again, and as we walk on, we hear Mama calling us.

"Hanna...Esther...I'm over here, children. I've been here all the while."

We see Mama standing on her hill, and we run to her. Esther will not climb the hill, but I must and when I reach the top, Mama takes me in her arms, and she smiles her beautiful smile, and she smells of vanilla perfume. She kisses my cheek lightly, like a tiny butterfly brushing past a flower and I begin to cry. She puts her arms around me, and holds me close. I feel her warmth, and I smell the vanilla and then she rocks me as if I were a tiny child in her arms. She rocks me and I weep against her breast for a long time.

When she finally speaks, it is as if a breeze is blowing past my ear, and she says to me, "Esther and Rachel are home, Hanna. You cannot come home yet. Someday, after you have told them your story, then you can come home."

"But I want to come home now, Mama. Please let me be with you. I'm so tired."

"No, you are only wearied, that is not a reason to come home. It is your job to tell them."

"I don't know if I can, Mama."

She holds me at arm's length and says, "Someday you must, Hanna! I want you to go and tell them what you saw."

I look at my Mama one more time, and I see the same tear that is on my cheek, is also on hers. I turn from her and walk slowly down the hill, and when I reach the bottom of the hill, I notice that Esther has gone. I call to her, "Esther...Esther... please come back!" But there is no answer.

I look around again for what seems like the thousandth time, and I see the sky is beginning to brighten. The barest pink is starting to rise on the horizon, and as I turn to go back to my hill, I come face to face with my worst nightmare. Standing in my path is Adolf Hitler and he is pointing his pistol at my head.

"Why do you run from me, what have I done to make you afraid?" he asks...as if he doesn't understand what he is.

I start to run. And I run as fast as my legs will carry me, first one way and then the other. Every time I stop to catch my breath, he is there in front of me, pointing the pistol at my head again, and again, and again, until I can run no further. I look around, and see the old man lying dead at the bottom of his hill. I see that the woman has disappeared as if she never existed at all. I see that my Mama is crying large, mournful tears as she calls out to me, over and over, "Tell them...tell them all...tell them..."

I sit on the ground and draw my knees to my chest and I bury my face in my hands and I scream...and I scream...and I scream...

80

CHAPTER XII

"Hanna...Hanna, it was only a dream. It wasn't real," whispered Silva as she held me close and rocked me. I shook myself awake, but the images of my nightmare remained so vivid it was hard for me to realize I was only dreaming.

"They're all gone, Silva. They're really all gone, every one of them. Somehow I knew that all along. But in my dream there was this old man, I don't remember his name. And he showed me the graves, Silva. There were hundreds of people in one huge hole. Do you think that's true? Do you think they could do such a thing?"

"You ask me that after what you've seen here? They are capable of anything, Hanna, you know that," she replied.

"Yes," I said, "they are capable of anything. And what I saw in my sleep?"

"It wasn't real, it wasn't, Hanna. Everything is all right, you're here with me now, safe and sound." And with that statement, we just looked at each other, and in the dark of night in building eleven at Auschwitz Concentration Camp, we held each other tight, because our very existence depended on it.

That night, I told Silva everything I had seen in the death house over the past two years. I knew if they found out, they would kill me. But I needed to share it with someone, and I knew Silva would protect our secret.

As I lay down again hoping for a dreamless sleep, I thought, *How lucky I am to have a friend like Silva. This much sadness is just impossible for one person to bear alone.*

#####

81

Over the next few weeks, I heard many rumors about the War slowly coming to an end, and that soon we would be freed from this awful place. But the only thing I saw, was the Nazis stepping up their efforts to finish the job they had started, in record-breaking time.

People seemed to be disappearing right before my eyes. Every day we lined up for roll call, and after three years of seeing the others gathered in the yards around the barracks, I became accustomed to seeing certain faces. When those faces were no longer there one day, it was obvious to all of us what happened to them.

The trains began to come more frequently too, in those last weeks of October and early November. I found myself playing the waltzes for eight, sometimes ten hours a day. Gruelling as it seemed to sit in the cold and play for hours at a time, it was blessedly welcome. Because, if I had to sit there holding a violin, then I wouldn't have to be in the death house counting shoes.

There were days when my fingers would be so raw from the strings and from the cold, that they would bleed. They never had a chance to heal, because after a few hours of fitful sleep, I would be back in my chair playing The Merry Widow Waltz once again.

The grassy hill where we sat and played was not so grassy in November. It was the beginning of winter in Poland, and that meant colder temperatures with each day that passed. Now, almost three years after I arrived, the winter artificial flowers were still there to greet the doomed. Ragged and faded blooms to deceive the unsuspecting new-comers, and very little sunshine to give them false hopes.

As I sat with the others, all of us wearing our blue skirts, white blouses, and moth-eaten sweaters for warmth, the blood from my fingers froze on the strings of my violin. It became a fitting tribute to these latest victims.

In the middle of November, a stunning announcement was made one morning at roll call. The voice of Rudolf Hoess, who was then the commandant at Auschwitz, came over a loud speaker saying that the trains would not be coming into the camp for a while. The orchestra was still to report to the grassy hill to play, so we could keep up morale among the prisoners. I almost laughed out loud to think that our two waltzes were going to do anything about the morale in that hellhole.

As Hoess continued to ramble on about things I knew and cared nothing about, I looked up at the sky and was instantly stricken by the fact that something was different. I nudged Silva and indicated for her to look up. After a second, we looked at each other and both of our mouths dropped open in amazement.

For the first time since the day we arrived, there was no smoke coming from the chimneys.

The ovens were shut down, and the camp was being systematically dis-assembled, so the German government could get rid of any evidence. This didn't mean that the killing stopped at the same time though. From then until the evacuation of the camp on the seventeenth of January in 1945, people continued to disappear. Gunshots were heard in the woods, and men were seen carrying heavy shovels.

It was around that time when I took ill. My physical condition had so deteriorated over the past months, from constant exposure to the cold, lack of sleep and food, and general lack of sanitation, that I developed a wracking cough and fever. It became increasingly more difficult for me to leave my bed and the irony of the whole nightmare struck me again. I had survived three years of this ordeal, and now when it appeared the end was so close I would probably die of pneumonia, alone in a filthy bunk.

On January seventeenth, all of the prisoners who were able to walk, were lined up with only the barest of clothing on their backs. They were lead out of Auschwitz on what was to be called The Death March. They were going to be moved through the woods, in the dead of night, to other camps, which were out of sight of the "enemy". Many of those people never lived to reach their destination. The only ones left behind were the people who could not move...the old, and the very ill like myself. Before I tell you the end of my story, I want to tell you about Silva...

#####

Just after dark on January seventeenth, the SS began going around to all of the barracks. We heard them shouting in the cold night air as they called for all of the prisoners to put on any clothing they had and assemble in the main yard.

As the people gathered their belongings, which were few, and walked into the yard, the SS began searching each building. They did two things: they destroyed anything that could incriminate them in any way and they shot many of the prisoners who were unable to get up and walk with the rest.

Auschwitz was a huge place, and many thousands of people were held captive there in the middle of January in 1945.

Besides the hundreds that were shot, and the thousands that were marched out of the camp, miraculously, 5,000 survive. It was either by an oversight, due to the Nazi's haste to evacuate the camp, or it was due to great cunning on the part of the survivors, but the ones that remained in Auschwitz managed to hide, even in their

84

weakened and dying states, and courageously perse-
vered for ten more days, until the Russians and the
Americans arrived.

I was, of course, one of the lucky ones. Building
eleven was generally left alone more than the others,
and on this night, it was somehow overlooked and I
lived.

"I can't leave you, Hanna. Look at how weak and
sick you are. How can you survive if I don't bring you
food and water?" insisted Silva. "Come, try to get up,
okay? Try, I'll help you walk. You can't stay here,
they'll kill you. Or worse, you'll starve to death."

"Silva, don't be crazy," I whispered. "This is your
chance to get out of here. I'll be fine. They never come
in here. And I'll hide when you leave, under the floor,
in the place where we hide the food. I'm so thin I can
fit in there easily. And when you're out, look for the
first chance in the black of night and run. Try, Silva, try
to escape. If they catch you they will end you quickly,
but it will be better than freezing to death. If I were
with you, that's what I would do. I would, Silva, I
would."

"No, you can't hide in the floor, they'll find you,
Hanna. You know they are like bloodhounds. They
can sniff out a Jew from two hundred yards. And, I
don't know if I'm brave enough to try running. Somehow I believe that if I can just hold on, this War will
end and we will all be safe. Now, get up, Hanna, get
up!" And she tried to lift me out of my bed.

"Stop, Silva...stop! I can't. Please, go now quickly
before the one they shoot is you," I insisted through a
deep, racking cough.

She sat down on my bed and held me in her arms
and we cried together. Sisters with no blood ties, but

85

sisters of the heart. Sisters whose love for each other had given each a reason to fight for survival.

I gave her a gentle shove so that she would go, and I said to her, "Promise me, Silva, that you will come through this. That you will go home with your head held high because you have beaten these devils. And, promise you will look for me, and I will look for you, even if it takes the rest of our lives to find each other."

She grabbed me again in a huge hug and said, "I promise." And then she left.

I was to find out years later, that the prisoners were lined up and marched out of Auschwitz with very little food, water or warm clothing. They were forced to walk 180 miles in forty-five days to Camp Hirschberg near the Czechoslovakian border. Along the way, anyone who could not keep up, needed to rest, or dropped to the ground from sheer exhaustion, was shot instantly. Thousands perished in this way.

Once the columns of emaciated, half-frozen prisoners arrived at their destination, they were allowed to rest for only a short time before the insane Nazis decided they were getting bored, and needed some entertainment. They made these already tortured people, strip naked and march around in the snow to German marching songs. A few days later, the still remaining few were paraded out again for their final destinations, small sub-camps, which as yet, had not attracted outside attention.

Of the ones left behind, we had yet another adventure in store for us. We had to survive on our own in the now deserted death camp.

CHAPTER XIII

When Silva was gone, I dragged myself to the far left corner of the building, and lifted the floorboards we had un-nailed, what seemed a thousand years ago. We did this in order to hide any food we were able to beg, borrow or steal. Everyone respected the stockpile. When the food was to be eaten, it was always shared equally, no matter how small the portion.

When I was sure, by the silence that there were no Nazi soldiers left in the camp, I struggled out of my hiding place, and crawled back to my bed.

I'm not sure how long I laid in that bunk, perhaps a day, perhaps three days, perhaps longer. I slept most of the time, and when I woke, I fought my way through a haze of high fever to the latrine, and from there to the water bucket, which was frozen over on top. With as much strength as I could muster at one time, I managed to break enough ice to ease my parched throat. After that ordeal, I would fall back onto my bed, exhausted from the exertion.

At some point, the people who were left, began to emerge, and I could hear voices. At first, I wasn't sure whether they were real or if they were part of my fevered dreams.

On perhaps the third or fourth day, I opened my eyes slowly, and when I was able to focus, I saw an old man standing over me.

"So, you live after all, huh?" he joked with a slight smile. "Wait, don't go away. I'll get you a bit of water to sip." And as he went to the water bucket, I too smiled at the silly thought that I would be going anywhere. He returned quickly, helped me to sit, and as gently as he would aid a child, he made me drink the full cup of water.

"I see you have managed to out-smart the Nazis also. There are many of us left, you know." And he made me drink some more. "My name is Mendel Horwitz. Before all this began, I was a physician in Krakow. You are very sick, but I think from the looks of your soaking bed, that your fever has broken. So, we will make you well enough to go home."

"Home? Are we going home?" I whispered, because that is all that would come out.

"Not yet, but we will. You'll see...we will." And he smiled again. "We have found some of the food supplies that were abandoned when they left. There isn't much, but it will be a feast compared to what they've been feeding us up until now. Some of the women are making a soup, I'll bring you some."

And as quickly as he came to me, as if in a benevolent dream, he disappeared again. I must have fallen asleep, because the next thing I knew, I felt a gentle touch on my face. I opened my eyes, and Mendel Horwitz was standing there again, with a bowl of steaming soup.

"I hope you like potato soup, it was the only thing on the menu tonight," he joked. I looked up at him, and whether out of relief that I was still alive, or because his comment struck a long lost funny bone, I started to laugh. The more I laughed, the more Mendel laughed, and the more my head hurt, until I was forced to stop.

This dear old man, named Mendel Horwitz, from Krakow, hand-fed me the bowl of potato soup and he continued to do the same, every few hours, for the next three days.

We talked, and we remembered, and we cried and we laughed. And of all the people I have known in my life, I believe I loved Mendel Horwitz the most. He was like my angel of mercy, my savior and I owe my life to that man.

At the end of the first week, I was able to get out of bed and breath some fresh air. I was amazed at how lovely the air smelled now that the ovens were not belching their sinful ashes into the sky. In spite of that, there was still the underlying stench of death and decay, it was in the very earth. But, without the smoke, there seemed to be a feeling of hope.

I dressed in my blue skirt and white blouse and woolen sweater, because I was certain that our rescuers would arrive at any time, and I wanted to look presentable. That very thought caused me to laugh out loud, but at the time, my thoughts were in such a jumble, and I was so tired and weak, that it all made perfect sense to me.

I sat with some of the others in the main hall at night and listened to their stories. During the day I sat on the grassy hill with my violin on my lap and waited.

When I try to recall my feelings from those days, I can't remember whether I was waiting for the trains to come through, or if I was waiting for the army to come and rescue me, or if I was waiting for the SS to come back and kill me. Very little made any sense to me. In my weakened state, it seemed very important that I just sit there and wait.

#####

On the twenty-seventh day of January in 1945 they came. By covered trucks, and by huge tanks, and by foot, they came to save us. I saw them approaching from the east and when the others saw them too, there was shouting, and cheering, and laughing, things I had not heard in a very long time.

The remaining prisoners ran to the fences and putting their arms through the links, waved at the approaching military caravan. Some who didn't have the strength or the ability to even stand, simply sat on the ground and cried. I sat on the grassy hill with my violin on my lap and watched and waited.

Within seconds the tanks broke down the heavy gates to Auschwitz Concentration Camp, and the trucks and men from the Russian Army entered. I watched as they ran through the camp, hundreds of soldiers trying to understand what they were seeing. I saw many of the soldiers take out their handkerchiefs and cover their mouths and noses to try and keep out the foul odors that met them at every corner.

I saw many of the men overcome by the sights and smells, lean against the buildings and vomit on the tainted ground. But worse, I saw many of these grown men weep when they saw what Hitler's army had done to these people. I saw it all as I sat on the grassy hill with my violin on my lap and waited.

I saw Mrs. Liebman run up to one of the young soldiers and throw her arms around him. She held him tight and kissed his face. I saw seven year-old Hyman Rosenbaum, being lifted onto the shoulders of another big, burly soldier. And I heard a child's laughter for the first time in three years. I saw the soldiers begin to carry out the old and the sick and gently place them in the covered trucks. I saw the others being rounded up from all corners of the camp and being given food and water. I saw a train pull into the station below me, but this time the people were helped onto the train and seated in the passenger cars as they were beginning their long journeys home. I saw it all and part of my heart sang with joy that they had come to save us and we had lived to see this day. The other part of my heart ached for the loss of my family, and my home, and my innocence, as I sat there on the grassy hill with the violin on my lap and waited.

Mendel Horwitz, my angel, finally saw me sitting on the hill and came to me. He sat in the chair next to mine and spoke to me softly.

"They have come, Hanna darling, they have finally come." He put out his hand to me and continued. "Let us go now."

"I'll come in a while, Mendel, my friend. I feel as though I need to sit here a bit more."

"But what are you waiting for, Hanna? We are free now," he pleaded as the tears welled in his tired eyes.

"I am waiting for the right moment. I will know it," I replied.

He stood and took my face in his wrinkled and warm, old hands. Those hands that for more than half a century had filled the sick with healing magic, but now only held the face of an empty girl. He leaned forward and kissed my forehead and said, "I don't know if we will ever meet again after today, my child, but it has been a great joy to know you. You lived when there was no reason for you to do so and you have brightened these last few days in a way I will never forget. Go to them and let them take you home."

I touched his hands. "You gave me life again, dear friend. There are no words to thank you," I said as I kissed his hands.

Mendel Horwitz walked down the hill to the waiting train. And I sat on the grassy hill with my violin on my lap and waited.

Something had happened while I was talking to Mendel, something different. I tried to figure it out, but

I was still so fuzzy and confused. Soon I realized what it was. There were other soldiers now, American soldiers who had come into the camp and were aiding the Russians in their rescue efforts.

I don't know how long I sat there, but the light was beginning to fade from the sky and it was getting very cold. I knew, in the still rational part of my brain, that I would have to make a decision soon. But what was the decision and why was I making it?

I began to play. Maybe that was the decision I had to make, whether or not to play for the people as they were leaving, the same way I had played for them when they arrived. I must have played for them a long time, because I finally realized it was very dark. Down below me, the trucks and trains were still coming to take the five thousand survivors to safety. I looked up and saw someone coming toward me, as I played The Merry Widow Waltz for, perhaps, the hundredth time that day. I had lost count long before. What I saw was a young soldier walking up the hill toward me. He was alone and carried a rifle in one hand, and he had a blanket slung over his shoulder. I looked down again and continued to play. "Miss, we're here to take ya' to safety," he said, but I continued to play. "Miss, can ya' hear me? I'm with the United States Army. This camp's been liberated, you're free to leave now."

As I continued to play in the cold night, with only the stars to illuminate my fingers, he put his large hand on mine to stop my music. "I'm here to take ya' out."

"What did you say?" I asked.

"I said, I'm here to help ya' leave this place."

I laughed and answered, "Where will I go?"

"Home," he said.

I looked down at the violin on my lap and said, "I have no home."

"Sure ya' do. Everybody's got a place where they were born, a family..."

"I have no home!" I insisted.

"Well, we'll just have to help ya' find it then."

My eyes were adjusted to the darkness by then and I remember looking at him a long time without a word. He was older than me, but not too much older and he had the nicest face I had ever seen.

"Who are you?" I asked.

"My name is Nathan...Nathan Weiskoff. Of course, everybody back home calls me Natie, so you can call me Natie too, if it makes ya' feel better."

"I'll call you Nathan."

"That'll be fine, Miss."

"Are you from America, Nathan?"

"Yes, Ma'am...Brooklyn, New York. Ya' ever hear of it?" he asked.

"Yes, I read about it in my geography book, before..."

"Yes."

"And it said that children played in the streets and there were flowers everywhere."

He started to laugh, which confused me, since I certainly didn't find anything funny about flowers or children.

"Well, you're right about the kids in the streets, Miss, but flowers everywhere is sort of a stretch."

"I'm not sure I understand."

"It's not important now, Miss. You're shiverin' pretty bad there. Let me put this blanket around ya' and warm ya' up."

He came very close and draped the blanket around my shoulders. I felt warm for the first time in months.

"Are ya' ready to leave now, Miss? They're waiting for us."

"I can't leave now, Nathan. I have to play again. They need to hear my music. I always play for the trains."

"Excuse me, Miss, but you don't have to play any more. They're gonna sign the papers soon. This camp is closed for good. Do you understand that? Germany surrendered and all these folks here are goin' home," he said as he held out his hand to me. "Please let me take you outa here."

"Another train will be coming soon, Nathan," I insisted in my broken English, and at this point I felt consumed by the confusion inside of me and all around me.

"But these are good trains, Miss, they're takin' the people to safety."

"There are too many trains, Nathan - too many trains, too many people. Too many children..."

I remember sitting in silence for a long time, hugging the warmth of the wool blanket to me, and holding my violin on my lap.

"My name is Hanna. Don't you wonder why I can speak in English?" I asked.

"I just figured you prob'ly learned it in school."

"Yes, when we were allowed to go to school," I replied.

"Well, Hanna is a very nice name. I knew a girl in my school with the name of Hanna," he said.

"Did she have red hair?"

"No, it was sorta brown, I think. Why is that important?"

"Because I had red hair," I said, and he understood.

"Are you a Jew?" I asked him. He nodded. "I heard there are many Jews in America. I will go to America one day. I will eat creamy chocolate pudding and read in front of...no...no fires, ever again. And I

94

will read in front of a window that looks out on anything but flowers."

I sat in silence again with my confused thoughts swimming around and around in my head. I looked again at this gentle man with the nice eyes and said, "Do you see what they did to our people, Nathan? They tried to kill us all, but they didn't succeed. They didn't murder us all."

Nathan Weiskoff sat down on the cold ground at my feet and said, "I know what they did."

I looked down at him, and in many ways, he reminded me of my Papa, but Nathan had an innocence about him that Papa never had. Papa had seen too much, had struggled too much, and had heard too much of the hatred against the Jews in Europe. That was something, that blessedly, Nathan would never have to face.

This man had a soft, kind face and I wanted to touch his cheek. At that moment, there was nothing I wanted to do more, than to touch his cheek. Because, in my heart, I knew that if I could do that, then everything would be all right.

Instead I said, "No, Nathan, you don't know. You can never know. You are a Jew from another world."

"Pardon me, Hanna," he said. "But, I know about the Jews and our suffering. We've been suffering for two thousand years."

I smiled a faint smile and continued. "No, you don't understand. They died, Nathan, they all died and I didn't. Why is that? What will I tell my children one day? How will I explain to them what happened here? Do you think anyone would truly understand?" And, without waiting for a reply, I took a deep breath and went on. "I sat here day and night playing my violin. I used to love my violin and I practiced for hours without Mama ever having to ask me. I loved the music, and I loved the place the music took me. Now, I despise the fact that I was ever able to play a note."

"I sat here and played, and watched the smoke pour from the chimneys over there," and I pointed to the now silent death house. "It was as if a thousand souls, at once, were rising out of those ashes and screaming their pain up to Heaven. And I sat here unable to scream. There is this enormous scream growing in me, Nathan, my body aches from wanting to let it out. It tears at every nerve in my body, every inch of my being. And yet still, the scream stays silent."

"I came to this place thinking I would be safe until the end of the War. The Nazi soldiers assured us that we would be unharmed if we just cooperated until we got to the camp. They said it was a work camp, they said that they would keep us very busy until the United States surrendered."

"They are very clever, these Nazis. They told us lies, and because we could not imagine beyond that, we believed their lies."

"The train, it pulled into this station where we sit. When they opened the big wooden doors, it was a beautiful day. There were flowers all about, and there was this glorious music played by young girls with violins, sitting right here where we sit now. I said to my sister, Rachel, 'How nice of them to welcome us so warmly. They can't be so awful as everyone says.' "

"They took my sister, Rachel, away from me that day. She was only thirteen years old. And they killed my mother at my feet. They shot her in the head, like an old dog. They took me to a building, building eleven, with other women. They gave me this blue skirt, and some salt pork, all because I could play the violin. They took away my family, and my red hair, and told me I was one of the lucky ones. And the flowers... weren't

96

even real." I laughed at that irony, but quickly my laughter turned to salty tears on my cheeks.

"I never saw my family again. They did it all to trick the people, Nathan, the flowers and the music. How could they have marched thousands, thousands to their doom without panic and riots, unless they used tricks? And me, I played a merry waltz as they marched my people to their deaths. How will I ever live with that guilt? They are all gone. They are all dead."

"But you're not dead, Hanna, you're still alive," he whispered.

I looked up through my tears and I could taste their salty bitterness as they ran into my mouth. "Do you know how they died, my family, all of the families?" I asked him, and he shook his head.

"Someday you will know what was done in this place. Someday you will all know."

"There..." I shouted as I pointed to the chimneys. "That is what they did to my sister, Rachel. She went into that building and only the smoke came out.

"On the day we arrived here, there were snowflakes flying through the cold air. We had no reason to question the snow. After all, that was God's work, was it not? And in November, snow is a common enough thing. But as the flakes began to land on our coats, and in our hair, and on our eyelashes, we realized that they weren't cold. They weren't even wet. And when I brushed them off my sleeve, I began to understand. It wasn't snow at all that was falling from the sky. It was ashes, from the chimneys. Great billows of smoke and ash, from the bodies of my people."

"We never knew," he said. "In America...we never knew."

"How could so many people disappear from the face of the Earth without someone, somewhere wondering? Is that possible, do you think?" I asked.

His answer was simple and perfect. "No."

"Do you think I will ever be able to forget this place, Nathan? Do you think I can ever forget the sound of the trains, or the color of the flowers, or the smell of the smoke, or the sobbing of the children?"

Again, his answer was simple. "I don't know."

We sat again in silence for a few seconds, and then Nathan stood up and held his hand out to me. I looked at him a moment longer and saw the sadness in his eyes. And then I held out my hand and took his in mine. He helped me to my feet, and with his free hand he closed the blanket around me tightly to keep out the frigid temperatures that had come with the night air.

I still gripped my violin as I looked up into his tender face and said, "Nathan, could you hold me for a second?" And without a single word, he wrapped his strong arms around me and held me as if I were a child. My tears came again in a flood, and for the first time in three years, I finally felt safe.

He held me at arms length then and said, "Too many things happened here before today."

"Yes, too many waltzes, Nathan."

He ever so gently, took the violin from my grasp, placed it on the chair and said, "Well, Hanna, you've just played the last one. It's time to go now."

He put his arm around my shoulders to support my bone-thin and weakened body and we slowly walked down the hill together...never looking back.

Until now...

ABOUT THE AUTHOR

Born in Ohio, but spending many years in New York and North Carolina, I now live in Richmond, Virginia, with my wonderful husband , Bob, our dog, Ari, two house cats, Blackie and Joey...and 17 homeless outdoor cats which we feed, and have had neutered with the help of a wonderful local volunteer rescue group. Between us we have four wonderful children and eight beautiful grandchildren. Can life get any better?

Now, as a retired Director, Drama teacher, Playwright, and Costume Designer for the past 30 years, I have won numerous awards for my plays, and directed or costumed over 60 shows in my career. I have also written 25 plays, which have won many awards over the years.

BERNIE BOLTON'S BIG APPLE CHRISTMAS, was the first of my BERNIE BOLTON BOOKS. Writer's Exchange has also published the second in the series, BERNIE BOLTON'S BROTHER. BOOK #3 in the series will be published soon. Also from WEE is STRINGS, a novel about a young girl's 3-year nightmare during the Holocaust.

I am currently working on a book of short plays which, I hope, will be published by Writers Exchange in the near future.

Find Sheryle's other books at:
http://www.writers-exchange.com/Sheryle-Criswell.html

Bernie Bolton's Brother
by Sheryle Criswell (Mid-Grade Reader)

Bernie Bolton was only a few short days from turning ten when disaster struck!

As she baby-sat her stepbrother, Kirby, the worst possible thing happened. Worse even than getting Miss Boggs for fourth grade!

As Kirby climbed a tree, and tried to touch the sky from the very highest branch -- he fell!

Afterwards he was in a deep sleep the doctors called "a coma".

Bernie tried everything to wake him, from prayers, which she wasn't very good at, to intimidation, which she was, to loud Elvis music and peanut butter. Nothing worked, until Emmy suggested visiting Mr. Ralston. He was the oldest person in the neighborhood.

His house was old, and cluttered, and kind of creepy... and it smelled like fish, lots of old stinky fish. It was also full of cats...everywhere. But Mr. Ralston made wonderful cookies, and had a mysterious, secret box, which he opened for the girls after telling them a story from his childhood. A story filled with wonder and a little magic... the kind that might wake Kirby from his long sleep.

http://www.writers-exchange.com/Bernie-Boltons-Brother.html

Strings
by Sheryle Criswell
(Historical: Holocaust)

This is fifteen-year-old Hanna Berkenski's journey from
her family's tiny apartment in the Warsaw Ghetto,
through the awful night she spends in a cattle-car with
her mother and sister, to her three years as a violinist in
the welcoming orchestra at Auschwitz.

The real horror begins as the train arrives at Auschwitz. Hanna's first impression is of a warm welcome
because of the flowers and sunshine and music. She has
been told she will be spending the next few weeks in a
"work" camp until her family is reunited and relocated.
Even the snowflakes make her feel a sense of relief...until she realizes they are not snowflakes at all, but
ash.

Hanna is taken to Building 11, where the "welcoming" orchestra women are housed. Her red hair is
shaved, her arm tattooed, and she is given a blue skirt, a
white blouse, and a violin. She is also given a gray dress,
which she wears when she is not performing. And then
she spends three years in Hell.

http://www.wriers-exchange.com/Strings.html

Crabbo and Clever Crabbo
by Wendy Nichols
(Mid-Grade Reader)

CRABBO: Ten-year-old Mark is lonely. He'd rather be at home with his computer than holidaying at the beach. But everything changes when he meets Crabbo, the talking crab. Together they take on the camping ground bullies and turn this holiday into the best one Mark's ever had.

CLEVER CRABBO: It's summer and Mark, Ellie and Crabbo, the talking crab, are on holidays at the beach. But Mrs Cripps is very unhappy. Fred and his mean gang are stealing from the Cripps' milk bar and the Cripps are in danger of losing their business. Can Clever Crabbo come up with a plan to trap the bullies or will the Cripps be forced to close their shop?

http://www.writers-exchange.com/Crabbo-and-Clever-Crabbo.html

Trambu by Donna Louise
(Mid-Grade Science Fiction)

Trambu came from the planet Voel. He had an assign-
ment. It was to safely observe other planetary systems
from his space mobile! However, Trambu's compulsive
and curious nature led him into an inescapable, swirling
journey to Earth.

Unable to return to Voel right away, his new mission
was to learn more about Earth. Is there a connection
between Voel and Earth? Could their statement, "Love
comes from the Heart" have another meaning? Follow
Trambu as he attempts to get some answers with his
newfound earth friend, Katie. Going to school may
never be the same for either of them!

http://www.writers-exchange.com/Trambu.html

20357681R00057

Made in the USA
Lexington, KY
03 February 2013